DOWN
ON HER
Luck

Down on Her Luck
Copyright© 2017 by Carmen DeSousa

ISBN-13: 978-1945143151
ISBN-10: 1945143150

www.CarmenDeSousaBooks.com
PO Box 253
Delmont, PA 15626
U.S.A.

Cover Design: Suzana Stankovic at LSDdesign

For any other permission, please visit www.CarmenDeSousaBooks.com for contact information.

Down on Her Luck

Alaina's Story

"You never know what worse luck your bad luck has saved you from." — Cormac McCarthy

Chapter 1 – Lady Luck Flees Town

To the extreme distress of my roommate — Joe was my boyfriend, really, but at thirty-nine, the word *boyfriend* sounded hokey — I'd spent all night practicing lines from the Broadway play for which I planned to audition this morning.

Joe walked sleepy-eyed into the second bedroom of our tiny apartment, which we now used as an office since I'd started sleeping in his room, and held up his phone, presenting me with the time. "It's four a.m., Alaina. Could you try to keep it to a low roar? I have an important meeting at nine a.m., and I'm almost certain all my neighbors are nine-to-fivers."

"Sorry," I croaked out. I smiled at the one word that came out as a gravelly purr. I'd screamed my lines, stretching my vocal cords so tightly that Eddie Van Halen could strum a chord on them. Now my voice was low and raspy, exactly the sound I was going for. If I rested my voice, it should have that perfect Kathleen-Turner edge I wanted by the time I auditioned. With my luck, though, I'd get to the audition and have laryngitis.

Still, it had to be done. This was it. My last audition, I'd promised myself. I was a tad older than most casting directors were looking for, but I still looked young enough. If the CD didn't skip right to my age on my résumé, he probably wouldn't notice, especially since the auditions were taking place in a theater.

For the last twenty years, every time I auditioned for a lead role, I was too short or too skinny. Too young or too old. Too tough or too feminine. Not this time. Everything about me fit this part. This was the role I'd waited twenty years to land. And unlike the last twenty years, I refused to accept a minor role. No way did I want to spend hours every evening waiting to deliver a few select lines. Supporting roles paid the bills, but they didn't feed my soul. This time, it was all or nothing.

After two more hours of whispering my lines, concentrating on expansive movements and dramatic facial expressions, I decided it was time for face-and-hair detail. Tweezers held at the ready, I scrutinized my reflection, inspecting my blond hair for any stray grays. I didn't have many, thankfully, but the few grays I had refused to rest silently among my other hairs. The wiry little sprites seemed to have a mind of their own, always popping straight up. I knew if I continued to pluck out the steely invaders, I'd end up looking like a middle-aged porcupine with thousands of hoary spikes, but I hadn't had the time or the extra money to get a root touch-up job, and the last thing I needed was to show up at an audition *looking* like I was over thirty. Made no difference that the audition was for a play with a title that indicated my age was perfect — if not too young — I still had to look younger than my thirty-nine years.

"Alaina …" Joe rapped on the bathroom door. "How much longer?"

"Just a sec …" I tossed all my toiletries back into my shower caddy, snatched my cosmetic bag off the toilet seat, and opened the door. Normally, having one bathroom wasn't an issue, since typically we worked different shifts. Most days, Joe was showered and shaved before I even rolled out of bed to make coffee.

Joe dashed by me. "Thanks."

The door clicked shut, and I ran to the attached mirror above our shared dresser. After I set out all my primers, concealers, and makeup in the order that I needed to apply them, I glanced up at my reflection. The black lacquer-framed mirror was large enough, but the lighting was better in the bathroom.

As a teenager, my best friend, Markus, and I had spent half of our awake hours either watching TV shows or reading books based in New York and had fallen in love with the idea of beautiful lofts with soaring windows and rooftop balconies. We'd planned to split the rent on an apartment like we'd seen on *Friends*, which wouldn't be an issue, since we'd been nothing but good friends. The two of us had had grand plans: he'd write the plays, and I'd star in them. But he'd stayed in Pittsburgh to take over his parents' real estate company, and I left for New York as soon as I graduated high school. I had never dreamed I'd end up in a shoebox-size two-bedroom apartment with three windows that if you lined them up in a row would be smaller than Joe's Smart TV.

Both my mother and drama teacher had assured me I'd star on Broadway someday, that I had that extra *oomph* that producers and directors were looking for. Sadly, my only *full-time* acting job was my day job, where I pretended to be overjoyed to serve food and drink to rich New Yorkers.

Even my love life was lackluster. Desperate for a safe and stable residence, I'd answered an ad to rent a room from Joe three years ago. He'd been a recent divorcé. He and his ex-wife couldn't sell the condo for what was owed on it, so they'd pulled the listing, and his ex-wife moved back to Florida with a contract stating that he'd give her half the profits whenever he sold the place. Joe had made it clear to me that he would never sell the condo for that very reason.

Joe and I had been attracted to each other physically immediately. And our personalities, while nearly polar opposite, had somehow worked. He was sensible and grounded, and I'd always been fun and adventurous. On our rare days off together, I tried to talk him into joining me on crazy adventures, but more often than not, he talked me into going to the theater. Then I'd try my crazy idea on a day he was at work.

Our relationship had gone from platonic to erotic in a matter of months, but in the last few months it had steadily dropped in temperature until our sex life was akin to a slow-simmering stew. I wasn't sure what had happened; it just got to the point where every night when I rolled into bed, Joe was asleep.

My book-loving English mother had always quoted John Bunyan to my sister and me, "Who would keep a cow of their own, that can have a quart of milk for a penny?"

But Joe was sweet, safe, and constant … and apparently, lactose intolerant. While his sensible attitude had turned out to be a tad on the boring side, his homebody attitude had never bothered me, because he had always been fine with whatever I did, and was always home when I got home. I loved him, but I knew our relationship would never be the *Romeo and Juliet* of romances, never the *I'd-die-if-you-left* kind of romance. But we were comfortable with each other. I just couldn't figure out what had happened in the last three months.

The worst part was that I wasn't even sure I missed having sex with Joe, even though sex had been on my mind more than it ever had. Mostly, fantasies that centered on Markus. About the one night when I'd returned from college and we'd moved our "just friends" status to lovers. Well, nearly. We'd rounded third base and then some, but the game was called before either of us reached home plate. Maybe if Joe had been interested in me, though, dreams of Markus … what might have been … wouldn't be stalking me nightly.

It seemed a cruel twist of fate that men wanted sex when women were too young to appreciate it, and then didn't want to have sex with mature thirty-nine-year-olds who couldn't stop thinking about it. Not that I wanted to leave, I was happy with Joe, but if I landed the part in the play, I should probably find a place of my own, since it was clear that Joe wasn't interested in taking our relationship further.

The thought of playing the lead in an ongoing Broadway show, the dream I'd chased for twenty years, sidetracked my mind from thoughts of Joe and made my insides churn with excitement and nerves.

"Bathroom's free." Joe brushed by me wrapped only in a towel, his dark hair glistening with water.

Another grievance of mine. Why was it men could be in and out of the bathroom in ten minutes and look good, but women had to spend an hour or longer to get ready? Before I could stash all my age-defying products back into my caddy, Joe strolled out of the closet, fully dressed, a tie around his neck.

"Do you mind?" he asked, holding up both ends of his power tie. I smiled at the red necktie around his neck that clashed with the flush of pink across his cheeks from his hot shower. His round boyish cheeks and hazel eyes might look sweet and innocent, but Joe was a killer. Well, killer consultant. I wasn't even sure what he did exactly, but companies brought him in to advise them, and then the companies did everything he told them to do, even if it meant firing half the workforce.

I reached for the ends of the tie. "Of course I don't mind." Years of helping my grandfather after his hands had begun to shake uncontrollably due to Parkinson's had made me a master at tying neckties. I adjusted the tie around his neck. "What do you have going on today?" Joe hadn't mentioned that he had an important meeting. Well, not before four a.m. this morning, he hadn't.

The muscles in Joe's neck tensed. "The boys upstairs have been keeping it hush-hush. Just said they wanted to meet with me today." As if he'd thought of something funny, his shoulders shook. "It's Friday, though. I instruct my clients to do their firing and layoffs on Fridays, giving employees a chance to calm down over the weekend."

My eyes shot up to Joe's face, but he was smiling. I smacked him on the chest. "Well, break a leg," I offered, using the idiom I would have used to send off one of my co-stars, but I figured it'd work in a promotion situation too. After all, I certainly didn't want Joe to lose his job. If he got fired and I didn't land the role, where would we be?

He may have lost his sex drive, but we made good roommates. Except when I was running lines all night and hogging the bathroom. But again, I reminded myself, this was my final shot. If I didn't land this role, I would take advantage of my English degree and find a teaching job. Thankfully, my grandfather had recommended not putting all my eggs in one basket, and he had been a successful businessman, so I'd listened.

Joe ran his fingers over my bare shoulder, sending a tingle through me I hadn't felt from him in months. "You too, Alaina. You sounded excellent. They'd be fools not to offer you the part."

I sighed, wondering where that had come from. It wasn't like Joe to be in tune with my thoughts. Other than sex, we really didn't have too much in common. Probably the reason we were good roommates for each other. We worked opposite shifts, enjoyed different pastimes.

He bent down and kissed me on the forehead, then pulled back. "Whatever happens ..." he paused, holding my eyes, "know that you're better than what you give yourself credit." He dropped his arms and left the room.

I peered around the wall, watching as he scooped his wallet, phone, and keys off the counter.

Whatever happens? Maybe Joe cared more than he let on. Maybe he was just stressed with work and a possible promotion — or worse, the possibility of being fired.

Confused, but not wanting to dwell on his feelings, or how his feelings might affect my feelings, I sprinted to the master bedroom closet. I couldn't afford to lose my focus today.

The master closet was one of the largest rooms in the tiny apartment, which was good, since Joe had more clothes than any man I'd ever known. Not that I could tell one dress shirt from another, or a sports coat from a suit jacket. Other than different colors, they all looked pretty much the same to me, except for the few items that were on the far end of the rod. Those few dust-covered articles of clothing were gifts I'd bought for Joe. Casual shirts and jeans that I thought would look great on him, but he didn't care for obviously, since he never wore them.

The phone on the nightstand rang as soon as I headed to my small section of clothes. I whipped around and stared at the ringing beast, not wanting to answer it. Whenever I wanted the phone to ring with news of a starring role, it remained noiseless. Whenever I was in a hurry, though, the evil plastic thing taunted me, making my hope soar ever so slightly. Then my confidence would crash when the caller turned out to be a salesman — or Joe. This early, it was certainly Joe not wanting to come back up in the elevator. Probably forgot something that he needed and wanted me to bring it to his work, as he'd done in the past. Since he knew I was home, I couldn't very well ignore the call.

"Hello?" My voice came out as a soft croak. If I didn't stop talking, I might not be able to speak at all by the time I got to my audition.

"Hi, honey. What's wrong? Are you sick?"

My head dropped. "Hi, Mom. No, I'm not sick. I was up all night running lines." I didn't have time for a phone call from my mother. I didn't have time to hear about how well my sister, Raylene, was doing. How smart Raylene was. How helpful Raylene was. How *not* sick Raylene was because she took better care of herself. I loved my sister, but I didn't love how much my mother bragged on and on and on about her. It didn't make sense anyway. My mother was the reason I'd spent the last twenty years trying to make it on Broadway. The least she could do was be proud of my few accomplishments. But every time I told her about a commercial or TV part, she'd say, "That's nice, dear. Oh, did I tell you what Raylene ..."

"Well?" my mother's voice broke me from my thoughts.

Damn ... she'd asked me a question after she asked if I was sick. "Sorry, Mom. I'm also in a hurry, so I was trying to dress while I listened. What did you say?"

"I asked if you were going to come home for Thanksgiving."

"Mom ..." I whined. I wasn't usually whiny, but my mother seemed to have that effect on me. "It's a nine-hour trip by train, and I really don't have the money."

"I'll send you the money."

"You don't have the extra money, either," I reminded her. Last time we had talked she'd mentioned that she'd be lucky to keep the shop going for another year. "Plus, I doubt I can get the time off. The restaurant is scheduled to be open on Thanksgiving."

My mother clucked her tongue. "You're waiting tables. How hard can it be to find another waitressing job? I really think you should come home for Thanksgiving, Laina. You haven't spent a holiday here in years. Ray and I miss you and want to spend the day with you."

I shook my head, wanting to say, *I'm sorry I'm such a disappointment to you.* But I bit down on my lip because I loved my mother and sister, and it *had* been too long since I'd spent a holiday with them. And it wasn't often that my mother asked me to do anything. Something about her request, while she'd tried to keep it light, told me she *really* wanted me to be there. "I miss you too, Mom. I'll see what I can do."

"Thank you, honey. Okay. I know you're in a hurry. Call me as soon as you make your reservations." And she hung up.

Somehow, my mother missed the, *I'll see what I can do*, and heard, *I'll do it.* But that was my mother. She was the boss, and she'd always been the boss. Her two daughters had, after all, been her employees for many years. I was surprised she hadn't gone with her usual, "And since both of you refuse to give me grandkids, the least you could do is succumb to my whims once and a while."

I took one last look in the mirror and was shocked to see that, with my lips pursed after the conversation with my mother, I looked like her. *Gah!* When did that happen? Oh, no! How would I ever land a lead role if I looked like my mother? Not that my mother wasn't pretty; she was. But I wasn't supposed to look like her for another twenty-three years.

A glance at the clock had me sprinting back into the closet. Great. Now I was running late. My thoughts back on the audition, I pulled on the outfit I'd set out to wear: a short black skirt and my most recent splurge, a winter-white, vintage-looking BKE top. I slipped into a pair of short black boots and assessed myself in the full-length mirror. Joe hadn't cared much for the outfit, said it looked steampunk.

"Good!" I said to my reflection. "Young, but not too young."

Hours — and countless young beautiful actresses walking past me to audition — later, I was not surprised to hear, "Thanks ... We'll let you know ..." within seconds of my reading from the script.

I wanted to throw the pages off the stage. To tell the pompous jerk, who hadn't even looked up from his smartphone once, "No, you won't let me know, so why bother lying?"

Ugh! Was there anything worse a woman could do than to repeatedly set herself up for a lifetime of constant rejection? What had I been thinking trying to make a career as an actress? Just because I'd played the lead in the high school play, had been captain of the cheerleading squad, had been voted most likely to be seen in Hollywood, I'd thought that I actually had what it took to be famous. But it was all a farce. I'd tried to cheat. Tried to skirt years of working for unpaid overtime, working through lunches, showing up on my day off when an employee was sick. All the things my sister had done to work her way up in her career. Now I'd received my reward. Twenty years with nothing to show for my life, and now, with whatever job I chose, I would be starting at the bottom.

And worst of all, I was feeling sorry for myself. *Double ugh!* "Snap out of it, Laina!" I shouted at the mirror in the ladies' room.

One of the beautiful young ones walked into the washroom at the same time I'd screamed at myself. She smiled, though, and said, "I like your top."

Only another actress — or maybe it was because we were in New York — wouldn't think a woman screaming at herself in a public restroom was crazy.

"Thanks," I said. The woman seemed genuine, a rare feature. "How'd your audition go?"

She shrugged. "Not sure. Got the typical, 'We'll let you know.' How 'bout you? You fit the part perfectly."

I laughed. See? Why didn't the casting director see that? Instead of announcing an open audition, why didn't the CD just post: *Twenty-somethings only, 105 pounds soaking wet, specific hair, eye color … everyone else needn't bother to audition.* That would save him, me, and the rest of the wannabes in the world a lot of time.

"Same 'We'll let you know.' I'm pretty sure CDs get special training on how to say those four words in every language," I said to the young woman, and then headed off to my day job, thinking that would have been a good comment from the haughty casting director, too: "Don't quit your day job, Alaina Ackerman."

I tugged on the long metal bar for the restaurant, but my hand slipped off when the normally-unlocked glass door didn't budge.

"What the —" I cupped my hand over my eyes as I tried to see inside the restaurant. It was dark. Not a soul inside. My eyes slid to a white poster board taped to the inside of the glass. In bold black Sharpie, the words OUT OF BUSINESS were sloppily written.

"Out of business?" I glanced around, hoping someone could enlighten me but, as usual, New Yorkers sprinted by, paying me no attention.

I covered my eyes, rubbing my temples, and sank back against the brick wall. Now I couldn't even concentrate on taking the state exam so I could apply for a teaching position. Instead, I would need to find another crappy waitressing job. And contrary to what my mother believed, it wasn't easy to find another waitressing job. Not a good one, anyway.

Not sure where to start, I headed in the direction of the apartment. Normally I would take a taxi or, if I had time to plan, use my Uber app, but the walk would do me good. And apparently, I needed to start pinching pennies. I glanced down at the blouse the other actress had complimented, thinking I should probably return it.

I hadn't dressed for walking outside, but hopefully the heavens would have mercy on me today. It was warm for November, but I knew that clouds held in the city heat, and clouds meant rain.

Within seconds of my thought, I felt the first drop. "Are you kidding me?" I grumbled to the sky. I envisioned my not-so-fairy fairy godmother holding up a clapperboard and yelling "action" at the not-so-happy fairytale moments in my life.

An hour later, I'd made the three-mile trek home. The full downpour had held off until I was within sprinting distance of my building.

Feeling like a drowned rat who'd also lost her last piece of cheese, I bolted out of the elevator, wanting only to take a hot bath and go back to bed. I skidded to a stop as Joe stepped out of our apartment, suitcase in hand.

He exhaled a long breath. "Hey … I didn't have any notice, but I left you a note, Alaina."

"Where … where are you going?" I said through chattering teeth.

The corners of Joe's lips lifted, then fell. "They want me to take a position in Chicago, so they're flying me out immediately."

"A position in Chicago? When did that happen?"

"It's a promotion. A good one. I didn't think it'd happen, so I didn't bother to mention it."

In other words, just as I thought this morning, *You're not important enough to me, Alaina, so I made a decision for my life without you.* "Oh," was all I said, though.

Joe rolled his luggage toward me. "They have a furnished executive apartment ready for me to move in." He paused to look at me, but I didn't know what to say. "Also," he continued, "my company is bringing up a manager from Orlando, so they asked me to lease my condo to him in exchange for the apartment in Chicago —"

"Excuse me, what?" I didn't even know how to finish my question, so I let my "what" hang out there, apparently the way he planned to leave me hanging out to freeze to death in New York in November.

"Come with me, Alaina. You'll like Chicago."

No, I wouldn't, and Joe knew it. I hated Chicago. Every time I'd gone on a business trip with him to Chicago, I couldn't wait to get back to New York. Every day was drearier than the last. "I can't go …"

His eyes widened. "Did you get the part?"

That would be the only reason I'd stay in New York, I guessed. Because, after all, what else did I have here, in his opinion. In my mother's opinion, too, apparently.

"Yes," I lied. I wasn't even sure why, but I didn't want to be anyone's hard-luck case. "How soon will the man from Orlando be moving in?"

"Not until next month."

"And if I hadn't landed the role?"

"You could come to Chicago with me …"

And there it was. Joe didn't really want me to go with him, but I could go — if I was happy with the status quo. Happy being in a roommate-with-benefits relationship. If I were desperate … I wasn't. Not yet. Not ever.

"Thanks, Joe, but no thanks." I wrapped my arms around my midriff and moved away from him, walking toward the front door of *his* apartment. At least I didn't have much to pack. All of my large items had been in storage since I'd moved in with Joe. I'd brought nothing but my clothes and toiletries.

"Alaina …"

I turned to look at him, but he hadn't moved from his position next to the elevator.

"Good bye, Joe."

He nodded and pushed the down arrow.

I unlocked the door and hurried inside. The letter Joe had mentioned was resting on the bar that separated the kitchen from the living area, the same spot where Joe discarded his keys, wallet, phone — and, apparently, his breakup letters — the moment he came home from work. Always the professional, Joe had neatly written my name on the outside of the legal-size envelope. I stuffed it into my satchel without bothering to read it.

Why bother? He'd been able to deliver the news first-hand. The idea that he would just move on and only leave me a letter made my blood boil. Besides, I didn't have time to read how little I meant to him. If I hurried, I might be able to catch the four o'clock train to Pittsburgh. At least my mother would be happy.

Chapter 2 – Coming Home

As soon as I stepped off the train, I heard my name shouted. I turned my head, looking for the source of the familiar voice. I had told my mother I would catch a ride via the Uber app, that she didn't need to be at the train station at midnight.

"Over here, Laina!" my mother called again.

I rolled my one piece of luggage behind me. "Hi, Mom. You didn't have to —"

She squeezed off my words. "No worries. Ray drove. She's bringing the car around. Her *new* car …"

Of course. And of course, *Raylene* would have driven Mom. Can't let Mom drive into town alone. Can't let Mom be left alone. And now Raylene would be upset with me because she had to drive Mom to the station at midnight and still get up before the crack of dawn. Loyal, dedicated Raylene also never skipped her exercise routine before work every day. Whereas I was barely in REM sleep at five a.m., she would be running on an elliptical or doing her Pilates routine.

My mother wrapped her arms around my waist. At least she seemed genuinely happy to have me here. I felt like the prodigal child. Next, she'd roast the fattened calf and invite the neighbors for a party. Oh, wait. Not veal — we'd have turkey. For Thanksgiving the following week. Yes, Raylene would be in a great mood, I was certain.

"Guess what, Laina?"

We hadn't even gotten in the car, and the twenty questions were starting. "Not a clue, Mom."

"You know that book Ray and I loved …"

I laughed. "You and Ray like lots of books." I loved to read too, but rarely was I interested in the books my mother and sister enjoyed. Although they typically were not alike in most aspects, they loved the same types of books, mainly self-help books and tearjerkers, books that I ended up throwing across the room about halfway through. I couldn't take them emotionally. I didn't mind shedding a tear when I read a book or watched a movie; I just didn't want to cry for days. I didn't care what anyone said; I liked happily-ever-afters. I liked to maintain the foolish *hope* that somewhere in this universe things might actually work out, even if that wasn't the case in my life.

"The one I sent you," my mother continued, "*You Don't Need a Man.*"

"Oh, that one." I was almost positive I'd buried it in the bottom drawer of my dresser, beneath the lingerie I hadn't worn in what seemed like a lifetime. The title of the book alone had told me I wouldn't enjoy it, so I'd stashed it away, thinking Joe wouldn't be too keen on my reading a man-bashing book. Then again, maybe Joe deserved some man-bashing since he'd been a coward. Who leaves a three-year relationship via a letter?

But the last thing I wanted to do was offend my mother within minutes of my arrival. It usually took at least a day or so until we started throwing baleful glares and sneers. Maybe I should have read the book. I heard the girls at the restaurant going on and on about it, and that Hollywood hottie himself Howard Edwards the Second was adapting it into a movie, but I'd just been too busy. "What about it?" I finally asked my mother.

"It's being adapted into a movie, and the producer is holding auditions right here. Well, not right here, here. In Greensburg. You remember that gorgeous old theater I used to take you and Ray to when you were young."

I couldn't stop the sigh from escaping. "Mom, there's no way on earth I'll ever land a role in a major motion picture. I'm too old."

"Didn't you read the book?" she asked, as if shocked by the idea that I wouldn't have read something she had sent me. "The main character looks exactly like you, and she's only a few years younger than you are."

Which meant the producers would want someone ten years younger to play the role. "I'm done, Mom. I'm going to take the state exam so I can apply for a teaching job."

My mother slowly lowered herself to a bench, her hand covering her mouth to hold back ... I wasn't quite sure what. A cry? A shout? "Here?" she finally asked, her eyes widening and glistening slightly. "In Pennsylvania?"

My own emotions spiked in response to hers. I knew my mother loved me, but she'd never seemed to care that I lived in New York. After all, she had Raylene nearby. "Well, I'm not sure about that ... New York and Pennsylvania both require a certificate, though, so I need to do some research. But I'd love to stay here while I figure out all that, since it's the holidays. Would you like that? Could I stay with you for a while?"

"Oh, Laina! That's perfect." She jumped up and squeezed me. "I'd love you to come home! You can stay with us indefinitely if you want. There's plenty of room, of course. You know that."

"Us? Who's —" My question was cut off by my sister's voice behind me.

"Hey, Laina." Raylene rested her arm around my shoulders and gave me a light squeeze. The kind of patronizing squeeze one would expect from an older sister. Next, I assumed, she'd ruffle my hair and call me *kiddo*.

My mother leaned back from our embrace, but lifted my hand at the same time she reached for Raylene's hand, making a ring, just as she'd done when we were children. "Laina's going to stay with us for a while, Ray! Isn't that great?"

My older sister turned her head, a half-smile lifting one side of her face. "Yes, that would be great." In other words, Raylene didn't believe for a minute that I was coming back with any degree of longevity. After all, I'd told her a thousand times that nothing would tempt me to leave New York.

"I'm just deciding on a change of careers, so I figured I'd stay with Mom through the holidays while I research my options."

My sister's lips turned up, and I wasn't sure if it was a, *See … she's not coming home*, or an, *It'll be nice to have you home for the holidays*. Without a word to explain her smile, Raylene — the most sensible, strong, and industrious woman out of the three of us — dropped our mother's hand and, with a grunt, picked up my suitcase and hefted it into the rear compartment of her Subaru Outback. Yep! Always practical. Always levelheaded. Right down to the new car she drove. I was surprised she'd even let a grunt slip out. Normally she refused to show any weakness, even a sound that a normal human would make.

Then again, Raylene wasn't like our mother — or me for that matter. While my sister and I could have been twins based on our facial features, she had inherited our Jewish father's olive coloring and no-nonsense personality, along with the same russet-colored hair and eyes. Clearly she'd inherited his business sense, too, since she'd worked all the way up to the position of bank manager.

Mom and I, on the other hand, have matching blond hair, aquamarine-colored eyes — according to my mother — and a complete lack of concern about the future. Which, of course, was the reason I was in my current situation.

My sister looked tired, though, and a lot thinner than she'd ever been. The six days a week she spent running the bank were starting to wear on her, it seemed.

As I reached for the back door handle, my mother shooed me away. "Sit upfront. You and Ray have a lot of catching up to do. You and I will have plenty of time to talk."

Raylene peeked at me as I plopped down in the front seat. "I'm sure you're exhausted, but if you want to get breakfast …" she trailed off, which meant she had no desire to prolong this night any longer than she had to, but Mom had probably suggested getting breakfast on the drive to the station.

I wasn't tired or hungry. I rarely went to bed before three or four a.m. And I'd slept on the train, so it'd be a while before I was ready to crash, especially with everything going on in my head. Coffee would be good, but Raylene looked exhausted, so I submitted to her unasked request by turning down her bogus invitation. "Thanks, but I'll bet I can find something to eat in the fridge. I'm sure Mom still cooks as though there were four of us." My father had died before I was six, so we'd lived with our grandfather, or rather, Zayde, most of my life. Every night, Mom had something stewing in the crockpot, and on Sunday, she'd make a huge meal that we all had to be present for. Even when Raylene had started college, she'd had to come home for Sunday dinners, except the last few months of the semester, when she'd been cramming trying to finish up one of her degrees. Raylene had only been a few hours away, at Penn State, so it'd been easy for her. I'd chosen New York, so I'd been excused.

A hint of a smile lifted Raylene's cheeks again. "Yeah. And even though Zayde's been gone for nearly ten years, she still makes his favorite meal every Sunday, too."

"I haven't gone deaf yet, girls."

"Not completely," Raylene whispered with a composed chuckle.

Mom unbuckled and then re-buckled herself into the center seat and leaned forward. "So, I have my two girls home, indefinitely."

My eyes darted to my sister. "You moved back home? What happened to Russell?" I knew Raylene and her boyfriend of twelve years hadn't married, but it had looked as though they would be together forever. They'd even purchased a house together. And why on earth hadn't Raylene or my mother mentioned this to me? It wasn't like we didn't talk on the phone.

Raylene closed her eyes for the briefest of seconds and then opened them, but kept her gaze focused on the road, where they should be anyway. "We're trying a temporary separation, so I moved back in with Mom. It was the easiest solution."

Mom tapped my arm, and I peeked over my shoulder. She just shook her head, telling me to let it go. So Raylene's perfect little life wasn't so perfect either. Not that that fact made me feel better; it didn't. I loved my sister. I just got tired of everyone telling me how smart she was, how mature she was, and asking me when was I going to settle down like my sister? – who apparently wasn't settled anymore.

At thirty-nine, I didn't need anyone to ask me those questions. I asked myself those questions every day now. The answer to all of the questions was … *never*, though. For me, it was too late for marriage and kids, and nothing I would ever do would make me as smart and as mature as my sister, who, I was certain, was born an adult.

Every year for the past nine years, I'd told myself, "Just one more year. One more year, and I'll quit." The words sounded like the cry of an addict. Maybe I was an addict. The odd thing was, I didn't even crave stardom. I rarely told anyone other than my mother when I landed great roles. I'd wanted to succeed for myself — and for my mother.

Fifteen minutes after we'd left the train station, Raylene pulled into the driveway of Mom's homestead, a three-story Colonial that had been built in the early nineteen-hundreds. The exterior of the massive home consisted almost completely of dark-red brick, had thousands of square feet, five bedrooms, four and a half bathrooms, a beautifully manicured yard, and was entirely too large for one woman. Well, three women now. Still, Mom should have sold it years ago. Raylene should have made her. The house had been my grandfather's, but even paid-in-full, the taxes and upkeep had to be a bear. The house was surely worth enough that Mom could sell it, and the business, and retire to sunny Florida or Arizona forever. At least, I assumed that's what sixty-two-year-olds were supposed to do. The majestic residence was even famous, since a painter had included it in one of his art exhibits about Squirrel Hill. She definitely should have sold it then. Then again, I guess it really wasn't my business.

Mom loved that the house was walking distance from her shop on Forbes Avenue, not to mention cafés, restaurants, bakeries, and even the Manor, a local movie theater that had been around for more than ninety years. She'd made it clear a hundred times: she was born in Squirrel Hill, and she planned to die in Squirrel Hill.

As soon as I stepped inside the house, my mind was whisked back to my childhood. The sight and scent of the dark cherry-stained wood floors that squeaked beneath my boots reminded me of sliding across the length of the entry hall. Raylene, who was only three years older than I was, and I would roll up the Oriental rug so we could slide the thirty-some feet from the front door to the back door. Until I inadvertently skidded right into the stairs, knocking out my front tooth, which meant no more wood-skating for either of us.

That had been when Raylene had grown up. Even though it hadn't been her fault — I was normally the one who initiated dangerous games — Mom had blamed her, citing that she was older and should have known better. While Raylene had always been mature, taking care of me while Mom worked. Comforting me over the death of my father, and later Bubbie and Zayde, this was the event that had transformed Raylene from a child who played, to the daughter and sister who was expected to be mature.

"Night," Raylene called as she headed up to her room on the third floor. The room spanned the length of the entire top floor of the house, but I'd never been jealous. My second-story bedroom had French doors that opened onto a tiled balcony that sat directly over the back porch, so it had been easy to sneak out of the house and shimmy down the wall after curfew.

"Night, sis," I called back.

She stopped and blew me a kiss, something she'd done my entire life. "Good to have you home, Laina. We'll get a chance to catch up this weekend. Okay?"

"Sounds good," I said, surprised by her sincere suggestion. Usually, Raylene was too busy with her job at the bank and hobnobbing with her longtime live-in boyfriend, Russell. Oh … That's right … she and Russell were trying a trial separation. Mom had shushed me when I asked earlier, but I was sure Raylene would want to talk about what happened.

Mom wrapped her arm around me and squeezed me again. "Come on. Let's go get some hot tea and have a little girl time."

Of course, I'd forgotten. Mom and Raylene drank tea, not coffee. I'd have to remember to buy some coffee.

I followed my mother into the bright white kitchen. She'd updated the cabinets, appliances, and fixtures after Zayde had passed, but I nearly laughed as I collapsed into the shiny red vinyl-covered chair that matched the candy-apple-red dinette that dated back to when Bubbie had run the kitchen. My grandmother had also been gone nearly as long as my father had. Zayde had said that she'd lost the will to live after my father — their only child — had died.

"Mom," I laughed, "you spent twenty thousand dollars on a new kitchen and still have Bubbie's old table? Last year you said you were going to get a new one."

Mom set the teakettle over the gas burner, and then plopped down in the chair across from me. "I just didn't have the heart. But haven't you heard? Retro is in. That's why I put in white cabinets. I like the red and white. So much brighter in winter."

I nodded appreciatively, even though the kitchen had never been dark. Since the room was situated in the back south-west corner of the house and had windows on the side and rear, the kitchen received plenty of morning and afternoon sun. Even the back door was almost completely glass, offering a splendid view of all the flowering trees my grandfather had planted over the years. Not to mention I'd sit here and watch Markus when he mowed the yard. I wondered briefly if Markus was still around. If he'd taken over his parents' company. If he was married with little baby Markuses running around. My mother and sister probably knew. Squirrel Hill was a tightknit community. But I wouldn't ask, since Markus was probably angry with me anyway. Angry how I'd left town the day after our one night.

Anxious to avert my mind from thoughts of Markus, I thought about my time in the yard with Zayde, how I loved piddling in the garden with him. How everything he planted was lush and colorful. Unfortunately, I hadn't inherited Zayde's green thumb. I couldn't even keep a potted plant alive in my apartment — Joe's apartment, I reminded myself. A hint of grief hit my stomach that, other than Joe returning my text to let me know he'd arrived in Chicago, he hadn't even tried to explain his leaving and why he hadn't mentioned the possibility to me earlier. After three years, I would have thought that he would have held a hint of love for me.

"So, what brings you back to Pittsburgh?" my mother asked.

Her direct question surprised me. My mother tended to be more subtle with her queries. "You asked me to come back," I reminded her.

One side of my mother's face pulled up as she flashed me a knowing smile. "Not that I'm not thrilled, but I asked you to come home for Thanksgiving and, as of this morning, you'd made it sound as though it were impossible. So, what gives?"

The kettle whistled, allowing me a brief stay of execution. I really didn't want to confess that I'd come home because I wasn't sure where else to go. That I'd failed at my final audition; my worthless job had gone out of business; and my boyfriend took off without as much as a longing gaze over his shoulder. It wasn't as though I couldn't have found someplace to live, though. I could have found something. I wasn't completely without means. If I were honest with myself, I had wanted to come home. Something in my mother's voice had made me realize it'd been too long since I'd seen her and my sister.

And I was tired. Coming home was the right decision, the smart choice, as I wouldn't have to plop down all of my savings on a new place. I'd have time to take the state exam, find a great position, and reconnect with my mother and sister again.

My mother set a cup down in front of me, then took her seat again, waiting for my answer.

I blew on the hot liquid, then chanced a sip, anything to stave off the conversation about my failure. I didn't want to admit it. Not to myself, and not to my mother.

She lifted an eyebrow, but then she set down her cup and slid a folded section of the newspaper toward me. "The open casting call is Monday, which gives you time to read the book before you audition."

"Mom, I'm done. I can't take it anymore." I dropped my head, ashamed.

She reached her slender hand across the table. "Alaina, this is your life. Don't give up now. Yes, take the state exam for your teaching certification. Get a job as a teacher if you want to, but never give up on your dream."

Even though I felt tears building up in my eyes that I wanted to hide, I lifted my head. "You gave up …" I regretted the words as soon as I said them. It hadn't even been an hour and I'd already started lobbing stones. That had to be a new record. And truthfully, my mother hadn't given up on a career in acting. She'd left show business because she'd gotten pregnant with Raylene, not because she couldn't make it. At nineteen, my mother had already performed several lead roles in local productions and had just landed a major role in a movie ... when she discovered she was pregnant, and the studio fired her for breach of contract.

Instead of being angry at my ill-mannered remark, my mother simply smiled. "And that's exactly why I'm telling you not to quit. Would you go to one more audition, please? For me?"

Chapter 3 – The Palace

The line leading to The Palace Theatre wrapped around the block and, as I suspected, hundreds of young women waited in line in front and behind me, each of them scrolling through their phones, oblivious about anyone but themselves.

As soon as a man moved orange cones out of the way, an all-black Town Car with dark tinted windows parallel-parked in a space directly outside the theater.

The driver, a slim giant dressed all in black, hopped out of the car at the same time the back door swung open. A woman my age, but with long brown hair that was swept up into a ponytail, stepped out. She was dressed casually and seemed nervous, even though she was clearly someone important since she had a chauffeur and an assigned parking space right outside the theater. I cocked my head as I suddenly realized how important she was. I flipped over the book my mother had given me. My mother had asked me to get the hardback copy autographed by anyone who was involved in the production. As many people as I could get, she'd requested.

The image of the author, Jana Embers, was on the dust jacket. Even with her hair pulled back and wearing glasses, it was clear it was the same woman. Mom would absolutely die if I got the author's autograph on the book, but I wouldn't dare shout out for an autograph while I was standing in line for an audition. As if it mattered. As if I had any chance with all these young women. I should probably just hop the velvet ropes and get the signature. Since it was a first edition, someday it might be worth more than I'd made all last year. At least I could say that my audition had paid off.

While I waited, knowing I'd never in a million years run after anyone for a signature, the chauffeur escorted the woman to the left-hand door, further confirming my belief that she *was* important. Strange that no one seemed to notice her.

The line moved slowly, like cattle walking across an uneven surface. At least the weather was nice. I had missed Pittsburgh's weather. No one ever believed me when I tried to explain that there were more "useable" sunny days in Pittsburgh than most places I'd visited. Even when it was freezing, the sun was usually shining.

Things moved along faster inside. A woman standing within feet of the door called people from the line and directed them to different doors. She didn't ask me which role I was auditioning for; she just had me sign on the line that matched the number she handed me, and told me to go to the door marked number one. At the door, a man handed me my *sides* and directed me to one of the remaining empty chairs in the room.

Once seated, I stared around at all the women, listening as they practiced and exercised their vocal cords. My voice was still hoarse from my screaming four nights ago, so I decided I didn't need to do any more voice exercises.

My scanning of the room stopped when my gaze landed on a woman sitting two rows in front of me. *It was her …* the lady I assumed was the author. Why in the world would she be in here? Or, was she just an actress who looked like the author, someone who'd been requested to be here, the reason she'd arrived in a chauffeured car.

No, if that were the case, she wouldn't be sitting in this room like all the rest of us. I watched as she listened intently to her neighbor, nodding politely, but then she turned her head away and buried her face into her *sides,* but not before I saw her cheeks blush scarlet. *What was she doing?*

The monitor called out a name, and the woman jumped up. I hadn't heard the name the monitor called, but I knew it wasn't Jana Embers; I would have *heard* that, since I had been listening for her name to confirm my suspicion. I was suddenly glad that my pride had kept me from asking her for an autograph. How silly I would have looked mistaking another actress for the author and asking her for an autograph.

Hours later, the monitor finally called my name and number. I started in response. I was pretty sure I had fallen asleep. After I'd read the lines a hundred times, of course. The only good thing about being near the back was that I had longer to study. Then again, the reader and casting director were probably asleep by now, too.

Regardless, this was my last chance. Really, this time. No matter what my mom said, I couldn't put myself through the adrenaline rush of performing, and then the let down as each hour passed without a call to come back.

The script was great, though. I'd enjoyed this scene in the book. The main character had been borderline depressed after her husband cheated on her. She'd taken up a few pastimes that she'd found online for free. One of them happened to be a self-defense course. She'd been late for class and had tried to back out, but the trainer kept her behind, insisting she work out her anger, and she had. It was a great scene … one I could imagine. I'd never been married, but men had cheated on me. And even though Joe hadn't cheated on me, he *had* unceremoniously dumped me for something better: a job in another state.

As soon as I read off my lines, the reader looked up at the man behind the desk. The man behind the desk, the casting director, I assumed, pointed to the opposite door than the one I came in. Many of the other girls had come back through the first door.

I was getting a chance to personally perform for Howard Edwards the Second, the director and producer of HELL productions, the man who made multi-million-dollar-budget productions. I'd heard the women whispering that he was watching the auditions today.

My heart pounded faster in my chest, so fast I could feel it throb all the way up to my temples. My hands broke out in a sweat as I turned to follow the reader.

I stood like a statue, careful not to lock my knees, though. I could just imagine doing something stupid like passing out. The papers in my hand shook as I took in the opulent theater that dated back to the 1920s, to the days of vaudeville and silent motion pictures. I was on the same stage where great performers in theater and music had stood. With its French Renaissance décor in rich reds and brushed golds, marble balustrade, spiral staircase, and black-and-white tiled floors, The Palace Theatre rivaled some of the most beautiful theaters I'd ever been in.

The reader motioned for me to step forward, but then I saw *him*. Howard Edwards the Second stood, his gaze connecting with several individuals, one of which was a tall blonde who exuded authority simply by the way she stood.

That and her thousand-dollar pantsuit. I also couldn't help but notice how good-looking and trim Howard was, way better looking than the pictures the tabloids posted of him. Then again, rag mags usually tried to make famous people look bad, as it sold papers when they wrote, "Look how such-and-such looks on the beach." Well, except when *People* magazine announced him as one of Hollywood's most eligible bachelors. Even I couldn't resist thumbing through the copy of that issue while standing in line at the grocery store.

Howard made eye contact with everyone in the room but me, then announced, "Have callbacks here tomorrow at ten a.m. sharp!" He took the hand of the woman whom I'd thought was the author and escorted her out a side door.

"What?" I growled, my temples throbbing with anger now, not excitement. As hoarse as my voice was, especially after I'd used every ounce of energy I had left in me to perform the scene in the previous room, I didn't think anything came out, though. Was I considered a "callback?" I hadn't performed for *him* yet. The reader brushed by me, back into the other room.

Not knowing what else to do, I followed the reader back into the room where I'd first auditioned. No way was I giving up. Just because Mr. Edwards was too tired and too rude to stay for a couple more minutes and hear my audition didn't mean I hadn't made callbacks. I'd made it this far, so they must have seen something in my performance.

I stood behind the reader, unwilling to leave until I had an answer. My arms were crossed, so I quickly dropped them. "Sir?"

My voice must have taken him by surprise. He jumped, then turned. "Oh, yes, Ms. Ackerman. Be back at ten a.m. tomorrow."

Tears rushed to my eyes at the fact that I made callbacks for a major motion picture. I immediately darted out of the room, afraid that he might see the silly display of emotion and change his mind.

The entire way to my mother's old Ford Taurus, I kept my head down, anxious not to make eye contact with anyone. Afraid that I'd burst into tears or a happy dance, I wasn't sure which.

I opened the door and fell back into the seat, my eyelids falling shut as I sent up a prayer of thanks. "Thank you! Thank you! Thank you!" I lifted both my fists and shook them, then pressed them to my mouth. "Well, thank you for the reader and the casting director. And if you're not too busy, maybe you could teach Mr. Edwards some manners tonight. Teach him it's rude to walk out on a performer."

Chapter 4 – An Old Friend

It wasn't the first time I'd made callbacks, obviously, but it was always exciting. And this was the first time I'd ever auditioned for a major motion picture. I imagined it felt a lot like advancing to the final round on *Jeopardy*.

"You've got twenty years, Alaina, how many of those are you going to risk?" Alex Trebek would ask.

"All twenty, Alex!" If I don't get this part, I would officially move home to Pittsburgh, I decided.

But I wouldn't make that promise to my mother yet. I'd simply tell her that I made the callback list. That would make her happy.

Thirty minutes of bumper-to-bumper traffic through the Squirrel Hill tunnel later, even without a single "tunnel monster" in sight, I made it back to the Pittsburgh suburb where I'd spent the first half of my life. In all the years I'd lived here, I couldn't understand why drivers hit the brakes before entering the tunnel. Even when an eighteen-wheeler was in front of them, drivers would drop to nearly a crawl, as if their passenger cars wouldn't be able to fit into the same tunnel the semi had. The city had even widened the entry, making the entry an arch in hopes to keep the traffic moving. But nothing seemed to work, so the locals had decided there must be "tunnel monsters" hanging from the outside wall that scared drivers.

As I drove through the streets of Squirrel Hill, or "upstreet," as my mother and Zayde had always referred to the area around their shop, a pang of nostalgia hit me. For just a moment, I allowed myself to imagine what life might have been like if I'd stayed in Squirrel Hill. If I'd acted on my feelings for the boy I'd left behind. I shook my head to clear it. The past was just that, the past. I focused my attention back on the shops, wondering why my mother hadn't thrown in the towel on her hardware store.

While most of the shops had updated their interiors and the products they sold, nearly all had kept the beautiful original fascia of their buildings. Many buildings even still had the names of the original companies carved into the brick or stone headers right below the rooflines or above the ornate entries.

Most of the shops around my grandfather's old shop, which my mother now ran, had transitioned to trendy bakeries, cafés, fine-dining restaurants, and pizza joints. Only a couple holdouts remained. Like the boutique toy store a few spots down, I wondered how my mother's hardware store could possibly compete with places like Walmart and Home Depot. Why she didn't sell the store was beyond me. Even if she didn't want to leave Pittsburgh, she could still sell. It wasn't like the store was turning a profit. It couldn't be. The first chance I got, I'd have to have a sit-down with Raylene. Mom shouldn't still be stressing out about keeping her father-in-law's shop going. It hadn't been Mom's fault that Dad had died, then Bubbie had died, and that we had been all that Zayde had left. It didn't mean that she had to work until she died.

I had to parallel park down the street from my mother's store, but the weather was a perfect fifty-five, cool enough to wear a sweater and boots without sweating — and yet, sunny. In New York, the sun would have already set, but here I got at least an extra half an hour of sunshine, enough to make it home during rush hour.

The bells on the door clattered as I pushed open the heavy glass door. "Mom?" I shoved all my thoughts about the store and house from my mind and plastered on a smile, knowing that my mother would be ecstatic, especially when I told her I saw the author and director. Who knew? Maybe I could get an autograph or two tomorrow.

I skidded to a stop at the end of the aisle as I saw a man behind the register. The bright sunlight that streamed through the front windows of the shop made it hard to make out his features, but his height and wide shoulders, not to mention the sharp features of his profile, communicated to my brain that he definitely wasn't my mother. Something about his face looked familiar, though. But it couldn't be ... "Umm ... hello?" *And what are you doing behind the counter?* I wanted to ask, but he looked as though he knew what he was doing as he busied himself with a shelf of everyday items behind the register. Was my mother tied up behind the counter, though? He didn't look threatening in his khaki pants and white work polo, but then again, neither did Ted Bundy. My mind still battled with the familiarity of his face, but Mom had never had an employee other than Raylene or me. "Where's Belinda?" I demanded.

"She'll be back in a little bit." The man offered me a friendly greeting as he turned to face me fully. I nearly gasped as I saw the face of my friend — the face that had starred in nearly every one of my sexual fantasies since our one passionate night — on a body that could grace any male fitness magazine. "Don't you recognize me, Laina?" he asked. "It's me, Markus Klein." The man who *claimed* to be and had the face of my best friend, Markus Klein, lifted the old wooden counter that separated the back area of the hardware store from the customer area and stepped toward me.

I tilted my head and smiled. "Markus? You can't be little-Markey-from-three-houses-down Markus?" *You can't be the boy who'd been there for me nearly my entire life*, I wanted to add, *the boy who'd grown into a man after high school, who I'd run from after the night* I'd *crossed the friendship line.*

"Yeah." He laughed, but his tone had an edge, as if he hadn't found my question funny, as if he might be thinking about that one night, too. "Things change. People change." His eyes narrowed ever so slightly. "You never called me that, though, did you? I'd always hoped that was just your mom and Zayde."

I gulped. "You've … grown …" Even more than the last time I'd seen him when I was home from college twenty years ago, and he hadn't been so small then.

He closed his eyes, and dropped his head, shaking it. "You can't imagine how many times I hear, 'But you were so short … so skinny … so, so … ugly …"

I darted forward and wrapped my arms around my childhood friend, then hit him on his chest, which was wide and hard as a rock. "You were never ugly. Who said that?"

He stepped back from my arms and shrugged. "Anyway, what's up? Your mom said you were back for an audition."

I leaned against the counter. "Actually, I came back to visit, and my mother insisted I go on one more audition. I'd already decided I was going to quit."

Markus scoffed. "Alaina Ackerman quit? Never!"

"I am … was …" I shrugged. "I made callbacks, though, so we'll see, but this is it. Alaina Ackerman's last stand."

"Ooh … I like the sound of that. Could be a book title."

"Right!" I laughed. "The day my life is worthy of a story will be the day Hell freezes over." I reached under the counter into the tiny fridge I knew was beneath the register and pulled out a bottle of water. "So, what's up with you? Last I heard you'd gone to work for your father, rolling in the big bucks via real estate sales."

He lifted a brow. "Do I look like a salesman to you?"

"Ummm … I'm not really sure how a salesman looks. Is there a standard uniform code?" I twisted off the cap and took a pull off the bottle of water as I tried to think what Markus *did* look like. He didn't look like the nerd-next-door anymore. His golden hair had grayed some on the sides, but his green eyes were as bright as they'd always been. And his build … dannnnngggg … Markus had filled out. *Would it offend him if I said he looked like a personal trainer?*

"I didn't mean looks in general," Markus said. "I meant … I'm just not salesman material. I don't have that killer instinct that my dad kept pushing for. If someone told me they wanted to think about it, I said, 'Okay.' And when he put me in an office … best to say, I wasn't excited about the prospect of sitting in a ten-by-ten cell for twelve-hour days for the rest of my life. So after ten long wasted years, since I wasn't willing to work my way up to manage the company, we parted ways and I went back to college."

"And now, you're working at a hardware store. Barely a hardware store, at that." As always, Markus wasn't offended with my blunt statement. He just smiled and busied himself with straightening up the counter, which was already in perfect order. We'd been friends since kindergarten, and he knew some of my deepest, darkest secrets and some other less-pleasant and embarrassing memories from high school, and especially after high school.

"Only part-time ... I guess it's only fair that you see how far I've fallen, since I know all your secrets. Like how you padded your bra to get on the cheer squad." Markus winked, and I shook my head at the fact that he had practically read my mind. "The hardware store isn't so bad, though, Markus continued. "It helps your mom, and I get a few fringe benefits. And more time to concentrate on what I really want to do."

"Which is?" I inquired, taking another swig of the cool water, wishing it were a glass of wine about now. It'd be nice to kick back with Markus and reminisce about high school and college life over a couple of drinks, especially since he didn't seem to be upset about my fleeing town after our night together. Maybe it hadn't been anything but a fling, something he hadn't thought about since. I wasn't sure how I felt about that, especially since I'd relived that night a thousand times in the last twenty years.

"Write," Markus said.

"Oh, that's right! I thought you'd given that up. What do you write?"

"Sci-Fi."

I stood straighter, cocking my head at this revelation. I'd never imagined Markus as a sci-fi kind of guy. "Markus! That's so cool! How come you never showed me anything?"

His shoulders lifted and dropped and, without warning, he looked like the skinny kid I remembered in high school. "Too embarrassing. All your friends picked on me enough as it was."

"No they didn't ..." But they had, and I knew they had. I'd never joined in, but I hadn't defended him the way I should have, either.

The bells on the door jingled, and Markus leaned around the aisle to greet his customer. "Hi, Mrs. Jones. I have your bag ready." He kept his eyes on the elderly woman as he walked past me. Stepping behind the counter, he rang up the order and then waited while the woman counted out the exact change, placing each bill and coin on the Formica top, and then pushed the money toward him without a word. Markus scooped up the change and handed her the receipt. "Thank you, Mrs. Jones. See you next week."

The woman left, and the small store seemed to have gotten darker in just the few minutes it had taken for her to come and go. It was so quiet I could hear the low hum of the overhead florescent light.

"So …" I started, hoping to cut the suddenly tense air between us. It was hard to believe that as good as Markus looked, he could still be affected by what stupid high-schoolers had said years ago. "Do you know where my mom is?"

Markus glanced at his phone. "She should be back in a few minutes."

My curiosity was piqued immediately. I hadn't asked when she'd be back, I'd asked where she was, but I decided not to press the issue.

I looked at my phone, too. Just a few minutes after five, which meant it was happy hour at most of the local restaurants. "Do you … umm … Do you work tonight?"

He smiled again, a smile I recognized from a long time ago, a smile that had put me in a precarious situation with my best bud. I'd been back from college. We'd both wanted to get away from our parents. He'd had a car and a couple bottles of wine from his father's private cellar …

"I don't have to work tonight," he said smoothly. "The shop closed at five."

"Well, um … do you have to work … ummm, you know, um, write … tonight?" What was wrong with me? This was Markus, the boy who'd been my best friend, why was I nervous about asking him out for a couple of drinks?

"Is Miss Cheer Captain, Drama Queen stuttering over asking a guy out on a date?"

I blinked. "Not a date. Just … a couple of drinks."

"Sure, Laina. We can go get a couple of drinks."

The bells rang again, and Markus and I darted our heads around the corner of the aisle at the same time.

"Hey, Mom!" I offered my mother a wave.

"Hi, honey." My mother locked the door behind her, then bustled down the aisle toward me. "How did it go?"

I bit down on my lip to hold back a smile, but she knew me too well.

She threw her hands over her mouth in response. "You made callbacks!"

"Yep!"

My mother wrapped her arms around me, and I noticed Markus retreat to the stairwell that led to the apartment upstairs. *Room and board* … I hadn't been sure what he'd meant when he said "fringe benefits" earlier. Apparently my mother was allowing him to live in the apartment over the shop. *How utterly author-like.*

My mother leaned back from my embrace. "Tell me all about it. I want to hear everything."

"Okay …" I shot a glance at Markus as he stood on the third step up. "But, I was —"

Markus shook his head, cutting me off. "You two have a lot to catch up on. I'll see you around, Laina."

Mom seemed to miss the entire conversation and just squeezed my hand, leading me out the front door. I peeked over my shoulder to see Markus just as he turned away and headed upstairs.

"Meet you back at the house, or would you rather go out?" my mom asked.

"The house." If we went out, she'd insist on paying, and I really didn't want her spending her hard-earned money on me. While my mother lived in a house that was probably worth eight hundred thousand dollars, I knew that any money she'd received after Zayde had died had to be dwindling. She simply couldn't keep up with the maintenance and upkeep on her ancient house and store forever. Maybe if I got a job I could start paying her rent. Living in Pittsburgh was sounding better and better every minute I spent here. Besides, Joe had barely taken the time to return my texts. He'd responded to my asking him how things were going with short responses: *Okay. Lots of work.* One text he'd said he missed me and that he would call soon, but he was just so *darn* busy he could barely find time to eat, let alone make a phone call.

Humph!

Mom hopped in her Ford Edge, which she had double-parked in front of the store, and I trotted off to her beat-up Taurus, happy she'd told me I could use it as long as I wanted. Getting around Pittsburgh wasn't as easy as New York, especially in Squirrel Hill where life seemed to be cut off from the rest of the world via tunnels. Before I lowered myself into the car, I glanced up at the windows above the store. Had I imagined that the blinds moved just slightly?

Yes, life in Pittsburgh might be interesting, after all.

Chapter 5 - Callback

The next morning I headed out bright and early. Early enough to get through the tunnels and actually have time to stop near the theater for some coffee.

Unlike the previous day, which had been an open call, Howard Edwards had said ten o'clock sharp, and he didn't seem like the kind of person who liked to wait.

To my surprise, a line of a hundred or so actors and actresses lined the sidewalk again. Thankfully, I'd thought to check before taking the time to grab coffee. I was early, and the line had already started to form, so I found a parking space and grabbed a place in line. The doors hadn't opened yet, so I found myself staring at the urns of coffee and other delights lined up on a patio adjacent the theater. Catered food for the crew, no doubt. My mouth watered at the scent of fresh-brewed coffee, wishing I had had time to grab some.

A few minutes after ten, a side door opened, and Howard trailed the woman, whom I was now certain was the author, Jana Embers, outside to the buffet table.

"That's him," a woman squealed beside me with a high-pitched voice that sounded as if it'd come from a thirteen-year-old girl. Her tone and excitement made it sound as though she were at a concert, watching as the lead singer in a boy band stepped on stage. "That's Howard Edwards!"

"Who's the woman?" the woman next to her asked in a whisper.

"That's the author," responded the teenager in a woman's body. "Jana something."

"Embers. That's Jana Embers," said a man with an effeminate voice. The man poked his head around me. "I heard she was going to play the lead in the movie. Can you imagine?"

I bristled at the man's comment. I *could* imagine Jana playing the part. Other than her beautiful bronzed hair, Jana Embers had nearly the same build, facial structure, and was the same age as I was, and *I* wanted to play the lead.

The women were in complete agreement with him, so I turned to the man behind me. "Wanna jump in front of me so you can talk?"

"Sure," he said as he sauntered next to the women who were barely twenty-something. As if they'd know a thing about playing the part of a middle-aged woman forced to take on a new life and career. Part of what made the story so intriguing was that the woman in the story had been cheated on by her husband of fifteen years, and even though she had no job, a fourteen-year-old-son to raise, and no idea how she would make it, she'd kicked him out and *found* a way. I didn't have a child to take care of, but I could definitely understand feeling as though I had nowhere else to go. If I hadn't had my mother and sister to come home to, it would have been quite a struggle for me. Not to mention I was going to have to start working on a new career.

Howard Edwards and Jana Embers talked quietly. Howard didn't look at the line of gawkers and admirers once, but Jana peeked up a couple of times, smiled shyly, then turned her attention back to Howard. How could she not keep her eyes focused on him? He had the most amazing blue eyes. I wondered if they looked as good up close as they did on TV and magazines.

Out of nowhere, Jana snapped her head back, as if Howard had said something unpleasant. My neighbors didn't miss the action either. They all let out soft "Ohhhs …" at the same time.

Howard looked contrite, though, and Jana seemed to immediately forgive whatever he'd said. An "Ohhh …" nearly popped out of my throat when I saw Howard reach across the table and touch Jana's hand.

Lucky woman … Not only was one of Hollywood's most eligible bachelors staring at her as though she were the only woman in the world, he was also adapting her book into a major motion picture.

Jana muttered something, then jumped out of her seat and charged back into the side door.

Howard stared after her for a second, but then whipped his head toward us. His piercing blue eyes made contact with mine, then his brow furrowed as though he were confused. Embarrassed by my gawking, I dropped my gaze at once, hoping he wouldn't remember me when I auditioned. I watched just his feet as he walked with a slow and easy gait back into the building.

My heart thundered in my chest. Howard Edwards the Second had looked right at me, as if he'd known me.

The three busybodies in front of me turned at once, their eyes narrowing.

"Girlfriend," the man said in a high-pitch that challenged even the thirteen-year-old voice, "Looks like HELL himself has your number."

"Excuse me?"

"Howard Edwards the Second. H. E. Capital I. Capital I. Get it? HELL, as he's called in Hollywood."

"He doesn't *have my number*." I laughed nervously. While Howard had held my gaze a fraction longer than was polite, he certainly didn't *have my number*. It sure would be nice if he did, though. That would certainly be helpful when I auditioned. But he hadn't looked at me as though he were interested; he looked at me as though maybe he knew something that I didn't.

"I disagree. That billionaire just eyeballed you," the man insisted.

With a huff, I shook my head. "No, he didn't."

"Ummm ... yeah he did," the woman with the high-pitched voice retorted.

Irritated with the three gossipers, I pointed behind them. "The line's moving."

The three of them shrugged and moved forward, but started mumbling amongst themselves. The entertainment business reminded me a lot of high school. It might be nice if I didn't get a second callback; then I could just start looking for a job teaching at a high school instead of feeling as though I were still attending one.

It was just after four o'clock when I finally got called up by the monitor. I'd barely stepped out on stage when Howard stood and said, "Same time tomorrow." He then wrapped his arm around Jana Embers and directed her out a side door adjacent to the stage. "Let's get out of here," he said; then, once again, he was gone.

I whipped my gaze to the reader, who at least had the decency to look embarrassed. "I'll make sure you're up first tomorrow, Ms. Ackerman."

It wasn't the reader's fault. Directors and producers were known for being eccentric, and Howard was both, the producer and director, which entitled him to do as he pleased. And right now, it looked as though he was pleased to be escorting Ms. Jana Embers out the door.

Back in my car, I glanced at the time on the dash and realized why Howard had probably called it quits so early. Traffic through the tunnels wasn't fun at any time of the day, but five o'clock rush-hour traffic was the worst. Better to be back in Squirrel Hill before the nine-to-fivers headed home from work, which also meant that maybe I could invite Markus out for a drink again.

Once again, Mom's car wasn't parked in front of the store. Good, one less conversation I'd have to have about my wasted day at The Palace. Weird, though. It wasn't like my mother to not be at the store; she must really trust Markus. I'd assumed that Markus was just watching the place at night, filling in occasionally. Maybe my mother *was* finally pulling back from working too much.

It wasn't five yet, so I tugged the heavy glass door open and strolled inside. I glanced up at the old rusted bells that announced my arrival. Probably the same bells Zayde had hung sixty-some years ago.

"I was just closing up, but if you know exactly what you need …" Markus popped his head up from behind the counter. "Oh, Laina. Hi."

Yesterday Markus had worn plain khakis and a white polo, which had looked fine. His clothes had looked exactly like I would suspect someone in a hardware store would wear. Today, though, Markus had on a pair of faded-in-all-the-right-places jeans and a black T-shirt that molded to every muscle on his chest and biceps. My heart rate jumped up a notch, leaving me breathless for a couple of seconds. Only because it'd been three months since I'd had sex, I reminded myself.

This was Markus, after all. The guy who, to my mother and grandfather, was, "You know, *Little Markey from down the Street*," as though it were a title he should be proud of.

"Do you mind locking the door?" Markus asked as he dipped his head beneath the counter again.

I twisted the metal lock and then rotated the rod for the blinds so that passersby couldn't see in. Not that there was anything of high value. Zayde had stopped selling major tools years ago, said that it was too much to keep in inventory. Instead, he'd focused on things the locals needed every day like flashlights, batteries, and lightbulbs. And items people needed in small emergencies like plungers and toilet-tank repair kits. He'd also kept seasonal items like ice scrapers for winter and charcoal briquettes and lighter fluid for summer. Not to mention a great selection of small tools and kitchen utensils. It seemed that Mom had followed his example.

Markus continued to shuffle around on the floor behind the counter, so I strolled up to it and leaned over. "Whatcha doin'?"

Markus peered up at me, his green eyes nearly glowing beneath the fluorescent lights.

"Awwww …" I stared down at the ball of cream-colored fluff inside a cardboard box. "Is she yours?"

"He, but no. I found him outside the back door last night. I'd heard a small whimper, but when I looked out the kitchen window, I hadn't seen anything. Finally, I went down the back stairs, and there he was, curled up next to some cardboard boxes by the dumpster."

Without bothering to lift the hinged counter, I crawled beneath it and waddled toward where Markus was crouched over the pup. "He can't be even a couple months old, if that."

Markus shook his head. "I hope he's just lost. I can't imagine that someone would have just dumped him on the street. Then again, I know that happens. Not that I have time, but I made up some fliers that I was going to take around town tonight. If he belongs to someone in Squirrel Hill, I would think they'd recognize him and call me. 'Cause I sure can't keep him."

I stared down at the bundle of fur nestled comfortably in blue shop towels I recognized as part of the store's stock. "What will you do if no one claims him?"

Markus stared up at me from beneath long blond lashes. "I'll have to take him to the Humane Society. I mean, where would I keep him? I don't have a yard."

My eyes widened. "But what if they put him to sleep?"

"Alaina, they don't put puppies to sleep. They barely even euthanize dogs unless they're sick."

"But if no one adopts him, he'll spend his life in a cage, probably smaller than that ten-by-ten cell you mentioned …"

Markus made a *tsking* sound. "That's not fair — Hey, you have a huge house with plenty of backyard space. Why don't you take him? At least until I find his owner."

"Me?" I bounced up on my feet and the pup bounded up from his slumber at the same time. "I've never taken care of anything in my life. I can't even keep plants alive."

"Maybe it's time you started," Markus murmured.

I scrunched up my nose at Markus, but then leaned down toward the puppy. As if the pup knew what I was doing, he squirmed up into my arms. "He smells good. Like …" I tried to place the scent. "Clean, like Ivory soap, so he must belong to someone."

"I washed him last night," Markus said offhandedly. "He was muddy and matted. I couldn't bring him inside your mother's apartment like that. She would have killed me if he messed up the wood floors. As it was, I had to watch him like a hawk, hoping he wouldn't leave any puddles. When I went to bed, I locked him in the bathroom, and he whimpered all night. Literally. I don't think I slept but a few hours."

"And you think I'm ready for that?" I asked, smiling as the pup tried to lick my chin. I'd never had a dog. Zayde had been allergic. Far as I knew, my mother and Raylene weren't, though.

"No, you're probably not ready for the responsibility. I'll put up the fliers, and if no one claims him, I'll take him to the pound."

"No!" I cried. "I mean …" The pup continued to nuzzle himself into my neck, trying his best to get as high as he could. "I'll help you hang fliers, and if nobody claims him … well, I guess I'll see what Mom says."

Markus leaned in and kissed my other cheek, opposite the one the puppy insisted needed kissing. "That's the sweet girl I know."

Humph! "When have I ever been sweet? Drama queen, remember?"

"Oh, I remember a time when you were very sweet. A delicious nectar —"

"Markus!" I smacked him on the shoulder. "I can't believe you'd bring up that night." But a rush of heat moved downward through my body. Forty-year-old men weren't supposed to talk like that. Joe never had, anyway. I'd known when Joe wanted sex simply because the six pillows on our bed, which usually resided between us, would all be stacked at the head of the bed.

Markus looked around the store, and then shook his head. "No one's here, Laina. No one can see you with me."

My cheeks burned. "That's not what I meant."

"What did you mean, Alaina?" He crossed his arms and stared at me. "Why didn't you ever call me back? Would you really have been that embarrassed to be seen with me?"

"Of course not! I had my life planned out, Markus. A relationship wasn't on my to-do list."

He let out a disbelieving huff, and then gnawed on his bottom lip. "So you haven't had any relationships in twenty years. Haven't dated anyone?"

"Of course, I've dated —"

"Then why not me?" he demanded. It sounded more like a statement than a question, but his voice was low and soft, his green eyes intently holding my gaze as though he were trying to figure out a puzzle.

"Because it would have been different with you."

"Why?" His voice went up in volume. "Because I hadn't played the lead in the play or been captain of the football team?"

"Of course not!" I said again, my voice rising as high as his had. How dare he accuse me of that?

"Then why, Alaina? Why were you gone when I showed up at your house the next day?"

"Because, with you, I would have wanted more!" I pushed the pup into his arms and ran out the back door. It was the fastest escape. I didn't want Markus to see the tears forming in my eyes.

What had I just admitted to Markus?

"Alaina, wait!"

I cut through the side alley and made my way back to the street. When I hit the sidewalk in front of the store, Markus was unlocking the front door.

I hopped in my car and peeled away.

What had I just admitted to myself?

Chapter 6 – Midlife Crisis

At the first red light I came to, I smacked my forehead against the steering wheel. Repeatedly. "What on earth is wrong with you, Alaina? Five days ago you walked away from a three-year relationship without even a tear, and now you're admitting how deep your feelings are for a man you haven't seen in twenty years? Midlife crisis. I'm having a midlife crisis."

That had to be it. Did women have those? Maybe I should go get some plastic surgery done like a normal actress who was about to turn forty. A little Botox around the edges couldn't hurt. Then again, maybe I needed to get psychological help.

Or maybe I just needed a little *wine* therapy.

Instead of heading to the house, I headed to the liquor store. A shot of the blackberry brandy that Mom always hid above the fridge wouldn't be enough for this session. I needed a box of wine tonight.

Ten minutes later, black box in my hands, I pulled into my driveway. As if wine could help … Instead of solving my problems, I'd end up with a hangover. As soon as I shifted the vehicle into park, I considered throwing the gear into reverse and backing right out again. Maybe I would just drive all the way to New York tonight. The guy from Orlando was probably okay. Maybe he'd let me stay there until I found another place. Maybe I'd get lucky and he'd be gay. A gay roommate would be perfect, then I'd never have to worry about moving out.

A tap on the glass next to my ear made me jump. "Argh! Markus!" I shouted through the glass. "You could have given me a heart attack."

Markus walked around to the passenger door and tapped on that window, too, a silent request to unlock the door. I again considered leaving. Then I'd never have to make eye contact with him again.

He bent down and looked in the window, then waved a handful of sheets of paper and a plastic box of tacks, which he shook. "You said you'd help me put up fliers," he said, his voice muffled.

I *had* said that. So, besides being a blathering idiot, I'd also be a liar if I didn't follow through on my offer to help. I unlocked the door, then picked the wine box off the seat and moved it to the floorboard.

Markus raised an eyebrow. "Planning a party?"

"Nope! I intend to sit on the back porch all by my lonesome and get plastered. Less embarrassing things happen that way."

Markus sighed, but then fluttered the fliers in his hand. "Let's just head up a few residential streets behind the store, and then the main streets. The pup's too young to have traveled far, so if he ran away, his owners have to live nearby."

Markus shifted the fliers on his lap so he could buckle his seatbelt. My eyes wandered to his lap … to read the fliers. He'd printed out color prints that showed off the pup's golden coat, then in bold black letters at the top was the word **FOUND** along with his phone number listed below the one word.

I shifted my arm over the back of his seat while I backed out of the long driveway. Reflexively, his head turned at the same time, and his warm breath, which smelled like the cinnamon mints he always used to carry, washed over my face.

Once I made it to the street, I shifted my eyes and body forward and headed off to the street behind the store.

"Pull over here," Markus suggested when I turned onto the next road. He hopped out, tacked one of the fliers to the telephone pole, then darted across the street, adding another flier so that anyone coming to the stop sign would see it. He darted around the hood of the car and hopped back in. "Head to the end of the block."

I stopped at the end of the block and waited while he posted fliers on both sides of the street again. We did the same on all the streets that surrounded the business section, then continued with a few more fliers on the two main business streets that flanked the store. If anyone in the area cared, they'd see the fliers.

What didn't surprise me was that Markus cared. He could have — probably should have — just taken the pup to the Humane Society. But he hadn't. He'd wanted to help. As I'd always known, Markus was kind. Nothing like me. Sure, I was friendly enough. Rarely did I call people names or talked behind their backs — unless they deserved it — but I'd never gone out of my way to help someone. I'd never even gone out of my way to help Markus. We'd been friends since grade school, but not once had I invited him to a party or asked him to hang out with my other friends when we were in high school.

As I thought about that, wondering why I'd never invited my *real* best friend to hang out with my other friends, I realized it hadn't been because I was mean that I hadn't invited Markus to do things with my friends and me; it'd been because I was selfish, but I'd also like to think, protective. I knew Markus was smart and sweet, and I hadn't wanted to share or subject him to others who didn't see what I saw.

"Would you mind dropping me off at the shop?" Markus asked after he'd nailed the last flier to a post.

"Don't you need your car?"

He slowly moved his head from side to side. "I didn't drive."

"How did you get to the house so quickly?"

"I ran," he said somberly, his gaze meeting mine.

I glanced at the box of wine. "Hey, that's a pretty big box of wine. Way more than enough for all of us. Do you have plans tonight?"

Markus turned his entire body toward me, the slightest hint of a smile lifting his lips, and shook his head again. "I don't have any plans. But ..."

"But ..."

"Can I bring the pup? I don't think it's right to leave him there alone."

"Of course. After all, I might be adopting him soon. Might as well get him used to me." I shifted the car back into drive and headed back to the shop, stopping right out front. Markus hopped out, and within minutes, he was back with a whimpering covered box.

He set the box on the floorboard in the back, then climbed into the front. "Wanna pick up some pizza?"

I smiled. He knew me so well. Not that practically every woman didn't love pizza, but still ...

He pulled out his phone and tapped it once, so he must have programed the number into his phone. "Hey, Mike! Extra-large with extra-cheese for carryout, please!"

Markus turned back to me. "Just head over to Murray Ave. Mike still makes the best around. Then we'll get this party started."

"I have to get up in the morning," I told him. "So, we can't party too hard." *Not like last time*, I wanted to add, but I didn't want my face to turn beet-red again. Had it just been the bottle each of wine we'd consumed that had had us ripping off each other's clothes in the front seat of his truck twenty years ago, or something else that I'd suppressed all these years? What would have happened if he'd had a condom? Would I have returned home after college instead of staying in New York? I shook my head to clear it.

He lifted his hands. "Hey, the getting plastered was your idea."

I shrugged, allowing that. "It sounded like a good idea at the time." But somehow, Markus had made the air between us comfortable again. We'd been good friends at one time, and then I'd screwed up by coming on to him twenty years ago. And then I almost screwed up again by making a stupid comment, by admitting that with him I would have wanted more. Thankfully, it was clear that Markus wasn't going to allow my embarrassment to get in the way of us being friends again.

Friends? Could we really remain *just friends* when the very air around us seemed to want to ignite from the electricity?

The ride back to my house was quiet, other than the occasional whimper from the back seat.

Markus reached his hand back and patted the box. "It's okay, Buddy. Laina's going to let you play in her yard. You'll like Laina's yard. It's pretty … lots of flowering trees and shrubs, so it smells nice too."

I gulped, then stole a peek at Markus, who had his eyes trained on the road, but I was certain I'd seen one side of his mouth quirk up.

Cheater. How could he act like just my friend and then make subtle comments like that? Of course, the yard was beautiful, but I wasn't so naïve as to not recognize he was being sly with his words, especially after his earlier comment about nectar.

Who talked like that? Then it hit me: Markus was a writer. He must sit around thinking up lines like that. My stomach seemed to drop a notch inside of me, wondering if that had been all it was, a line. Maybe to get me to finish what we'd started twenty years ago, the sleeping-with-him part.

I jerked the car to the left, pulling into my driveway, making Markus grab the bar above the door at the same time he steadied the pizza box on his lap. "Jeeze, Lain. You in a hurry?" He looked in the back seat, but I knew the box was fine, since it was on the floorboard.

"Just hungry." As soon as the car came to a stop, I hopped out, grabbing the box of wine. "Here, hand me the pizza." I reached for the box in his hands so he could get the pup.

Pizza in one hand and wine in the other, I hurried to the door leading to the mudroom, the only door we ever used. Only visitors were allowed to enter the house through the front door. I dropped the pizza and wine on the counter, and then went looking for my mother and sister.

Chaperones were a must tonight. Without my mother or sister standing guard, I was likely to either kill Markus or sleep with him. One would get me sent away for life, the other … I didn't even want to consider that outcome.

As I entered the foyer, I saw my sister at the top of the stairs. Although she'd said we'd catch up over the weekend, I hadn't seen her for more than a few minutes. Since I'd been home, she had either been at work, going to work, or tired after work and planning to turn in early.

"Hey, Ray," I said to her retreating backside. "Markus and I brought pizza and a box of wine. You hungry?"

Raylene turned and smiled. "Thanks, but it's been a long day. I'll see you tomorrow."

Did she just not want to be a third-wheel? I wondered. "Is Mom home?"

"She just left. Tuesday night is five-dollar-movie night, so she normally goes out with her friends."

Friends? I didn't know my mom had started hanging out with friends. She never had before. She'd never even dated after Dad died. Like Zayde, she'd just concentrated on the store.

"Night, Laina!" Raylene blew me a kiss and disappeared behind the wall.

"Night, Ray!" Markus called behind me.

"Night, Markus!" The sound of my sister's voice faded as she made her way up the stairs.

The way Raylene had said goodnight to Markus, but hadn't bothered to come back, made it clear that she and Markus were more familiar with each other than the boy and girl who'd lived next to each other for thirty-plus years but had never spoken to each other much. Raylene was three years older than Markus and me, so she'd never wanted to hang out with us in high school. Even when we did cross paths in the cafeteria, sporting events, or local hangouts, she'd always treated Markus as an acquaintance more than a friend. Had something changed now that he worked for our mother?

I turned to voice something — I wasn't sure exactly what — to Markus, but he was already walking back to the kitchen, as familiar in my house as he'd been when he was a kid. His father and mother had both worked nearly 'round-the-clock hours at their real estate office, which they'd grown to a large group of agencies in Pennsylvania, so Markus had spent a lot of time at our house.

"Come on, Buddy," Markus said to the box as he walked toward the back door. "Let's go play."

That was the second time he'd called the pup "Buddy." Had he already named him? I couldn't help but smile as I watched Markus stoop and lift the ball of fur out of the box and set him on the grass. The pup immediately squatted. That was a good sign. Markus had been right; Mom wouldn't be too happy if the puppy relieved himself on her antique Oriental rugs or original wood floors. Maybe that was why Markus hadn't pressed me to take Buddy full time yet. Maybe he'd wanted to train him first so my mother — who'd always been a stickler about keeping a pristine home — wouldn't get upset if Buddy had any accidents.

Markus and Buddy seemed to be getting along fine, so I headed back to the kitchen and went to work on opening the box of wine. As a starving — or rather, *thirsty* — actress, I'd come to appreciate wine in a box. It was cheaper, and it stayed fresh longer, which meant it was available when I needed it most. I broke apart the cardboard along the perforated lines and pulled out the spout, then poured two generous portions. Next, I grabbed two paper plates off the shelf, adding two slices to each.

With the plates lined up my left arm and the two wine glasses threaded between my fingers, I headed to the back porch. Markus darted up the stairs as I approached the storm door, and pulled it open just as I started to back my way through it. Years of waiting on tables had made me proficient when it came to balancing plates and glasses. Balancing my emotions, on the other hand, I still needed to practice, it seemed, as just the act of Markus racing to help me open the door sent a bubbling sensation up my chest, and I hadn't even had a sip of wine yet.

I knew Markus was sweet, but since we'd never been in a boyfriend-girlfriend relationship, and he'd never dated anyone I'd known, I had no idea how he'd treat a woman. I knew how Markus kissed a woman, though … I sighed at the memory, then lowered my head as though I were watching what I was doing so he couldn't see my face, which I was certain was as red as it felt.

Markus accepted a plate and a glass and took a seat on one side of the wicker loveseat. The pup yipped as he tried to climb the steps. "Oh," Markus said, jumping up to get the pup, but I waved him off, another means to keep my face out of his view.

I set my plate and glass next to his, then went for the pup. "Hey, Buddy. Legs too short? I know the feeling." Since performing on stage always focused on bigger-than-life actions, I had always wondered if I would have landed more roles if I were taller. Unlike in film, where the camera followed an actor's every move, stage performers had to make sure that the audience all the way in the back of the auditorium could see their actions. I reached for the pup and set him on the porch, but then realized I needed to wash my hands. I walked back into the house and came out with my travel-size bottle of antibacterial liquid from my purse. I wasn't a germ freak, but I didn't know where the pup had been before he ended up behind the store. Since I planned to eat with my hands, I didn't want doggie germs on my pizza, even as clean as he looked and smelled.

"Want some?" I held out the bottle to Markus and he nodded and accepted a squirt.

"Probably a good idea."

He lifted his wine glass to me as I sat down on the opposite side of the loveseat. "To old friends."

I picked up my glass and tapped it to his. "To best friends."

Markus smiled. "We really were, weren't we?"

"Yes …"

He sighed, which I took as a *Why haven't you called me in twenty years, then?* question, but he said nothing and took a sip.

Why hadn't I tried? I knew where he worked. Where he lived. Well, where his parents worked and lived. But I could have reached him.

I took a sip, then picked up a piece of the pizza. One bite in, I moaned. "Oh, this is so good." I'd been on a diet since I was in high school, but not anymore. If I didn't get this part, I planned to gain twenty pounds. "It takes me back."

"Ahhh … yes. Junior high birthday parties, when we were still ignorant of the differences between boys and girls."

I giggled. "True. Why are birthday and holiday parties co-ed until age thirteen, and then they're 'girls or boys' only until seventeen? What happens in those three years?"

"Because they'd be just like those dances our parents sent us to. Where all the boys lined up on one side of the gym, and all the girls lined up on the other, waiting for the boys to grow up and ask one of them to dance. Then when one boy braved crossing the gym floor, the girl would turn him down. Co-ed parties between the ages of thirteen and sixteen would have been boring. Instead, we boys played laser tag, and you girls played Truth-or-Dare at slumber parties."

I laughed, imagining Markus as the scrawny boy sitting across the gym, having to walk back to the other side after a girl rejected him. And worse, the stupid dares I had to perform because I wouldn't confess to my friends whom I wanted to marry when I grew up, since the only boy I ever imagined marrying was Markus, and they didn't see what I saw in him. "Yeah, I guess you're right." I took another bite, then searched for a topic change, as I was starting to feel a lot like the girl waiting on the other side of the gym right now. As much as my head was afraid of what would happen if Markus made a move on me, my body wasn't getting the message. Only two sips of wine, and my insides were already heating up as my brain flashed back to a petting scene behind steamed-up windows of a truck. "So … how did you end up working for my mother?"

The pup stood on his hind legs, his front paws scratching at the wicker settee. Markus nudged him away with the back of his hand as he softly disciplined him with a "No," then turned to me. "After going back to college, I'd landed another great-paying job that I hated, and wasted another couple years of my life. When I finally decided to concentrate on writing full-time, I needed a cheaper place to stay. I remembered that old apartment above the shop. I told Belinda I'd fix it up and pull a few hours of work if she'd let me move in. The last few tenants she had were nothing but trouble, so she hadn't rented it in years."

How had Markus known that, and I hadn't?

"Ray told me," Markus said as if he'd heard my thoughts. Then I realized I'd furrowed my brow and tilted my head. He really was my best friend. He'd always sensed when I was upset. "Anyway, it's working for both of us.

Gives your mother some free time, and gives me a chance to actually finish writing something for once."

"When do you talk to Ray? I didn't know you were friends."

Markus picked up his glass and took another sip before answering. "I bank where she works. If she's not busy when I'm there, I pop into her office to see how she and your mother are getting along … and to enquire about you."

I reeled a bit. "Enquire about me? Like what?"

Markus leaned back and pulled one of his legs up on the cushion so he was facing me. "The usual. Had you made it big on Broadway yet? Were you still single? And when were you coming home?"

Home … The word traveled through me like magma through a lava tube, as if Markus himself were home. But Markus wasn't home. I lived with another man. Well, sort of.

"Markus," I gulped, "I —"

He leaned forward, lifting his hand to my lips. "You don't have to respond, Laina. This is my hang-up, not yours. I'm just being honest with you, as I should have been years ago. If you don't want to know, though, don't ask."

I was almost certain my heart hadn't just skipped a beat, but had actually stopped beating altogether, but I hadn't even told Joe I'd left the apartment, left New York, because I hadn't known for sure if I was going or staying.

"I'm sorry, Markus, you know how much you've always meant to me, but I —" It wasn't right not to tell Markus that I was in a relationship. Again, sort of in a relationship. After all, Joe was the one who'd left. Still … "Did my sister tell you I was living with someone?"

His eyes shuttered, then opened, as if I'd hurt him. "Yes, but she also mentioned you weren't married and that you didn't love him."

"Raylene said I wasn't in love with Joe?"

"Yes …" Markus suddenly sat straighter. "Was she wrong?"

My heart raced again, and my palms broke out into a sweat even though it was forty degrees outside. "It wouldn't matter if Ray was right or wrong —" I shook my head. "Let's talk about something else, please."

Markus lifted his head slowly, then lowered it, then rubbed his eyes as though he wasn't quite sure how to respond. "So, how did today go?" he asked. "Did you get the part?"

I shook my head and tried to suppress a smile at his willingness to change the topic, thankful that he wasn't pressing me for an answer about Joe, forcing me to admit something that I didn't want to think about right now. "I got another callback. Howard Edwards the Second, the producer —"

Markus pressed his lips into a straight line, and attempted a smile, but it was short-lived. "I know who Howard is."

"Well, he was just as rude as the first day; he left before I could audition. But the reader, the guy who reads the lines of —"

"I know what a reader does, Alaina. Remember, that was my contribution to the high school play."

"Oh, right. Sorry."

He shrugged.

"Anyway, the reader said I'd be first up tomorrow, so hopefully, I'll know one way or another."

"And if you get the part, you'll be off to Hollywood, and if you don't …" Markus looked hopeful, but it didn't look as though he were hopeful I'd get the part. No, he only seemed to care about the question he hadn't asked, the one he'd left dangling for me to finish.

"I'm not sure."

His brows furrowed slightly, and I knew with almost certainty that his unasked question had been rhetorical.

"Have my mother and sister been giving you a play-by-play of my life?" I demanded.

"Not everything." Markus shook his head. "Your mom's just hoping that if you don't get the part you'll find a job as a teacher, and stay here instead of going back to New York."

"So the three of you want me to fail? As if failing for the last twenty years wasn't enough, you want me to fail and have to come crying home?" I slammed my glass down and stood. The pup, who had been sprawled out on the wood planks between our feet, jumped, but Markus remained where he was, his arm draped over the back of the seat cushion, and his wine glass clutched in his hand. "I think you should go, Markus. I'm sure my mother and sister will let you know what happens to me."

He just stared up at me, then shook his head. "Is it so wrong that we want you to come home, Laina?"

"If it means you want me to fail, then, yes!" I nearly shouted. "And you don't live here, Markus. This isn't your home."

With that, Markus set down his glass and scooped up the pup. He headed for the steps, and I remembered I'd driven him here.

"I'll go get my keys," I growled.

He turned to me, and his face was unreadable. Not angry, as I thought it might be after my ill-mannered remark. Instead, his face appeared blank, empty of emotion. "Don't bother. I know my way home."

Chapter 7 – Life Isn't Over

My alarm went off and I jumped, even though I hadn't been sleeping. I'd just been staring up at the swirled shapes in the plaster ceiling, replaying last night in my head.

What was wrong with me? Why had I overreacted with Markus? I'd said he was my best friend, but then freaked out because he was talking with my mother and sister about me. Of course, I was a topic of conversation between my family and him. What else would he discuss with my mother and sister? I was probably a conversation-filler while Markus and my mother traded shifts at the store, or when he did business at the bank. It didn't mean they were planning my life behind my back. As if anyone could do that anyway.

Clearly, I'd been the incompetent director of my life for the last twenty years. A knowledgeable producer would have fired me years ago instead of sending a once-in-a-lifetime major production like *my life* into bankruptcy.

In order to clear my head, I hopped in the shower before heading downstairs. I needed to wash yesterday's frustrations down the drain. Oddly enough, even though I'd been a struggling actress — most of the time — making a living waiting tables, and my love life had been lackluster at best, I hadn't been as stressed in New York. Maybe because I'd kept myself so busy I'd been able to ignore reality.

Since I'd come home, my nerves were on high alert, as if sensing an undercurrent of strain between my mother and Raylene. Heck, even Markus seemed to be pushing me, and he'd never pushed me in high school for anything. Was it just because we were about to turn forty? What difference did it make? It wasn't as though my biological clock was ticking. I'd *snoozed* that alarm one too many times. Now it was forever on mute. So, what was the sudden pressure to tell me how he felt? Why couldn't we just let things progress as they always had? If *it* happened, it happened.

After a long hot shower, I slipped into my only remaining clean outfit, faded jeans and a NY Yankees sweatshirt that my mother and sister were sure to rag on me about, as would anyone else in Pittsburgh who saw me. At least it wasn't a Browns shirt. Baseball fans seemed to be a lot more forgiving than football fans.

When I reached the bottom step, I realized the house was utterly quiet again. I peeked into the kitchen, and then onto the back porch, but seeing neither of my housemates, I decided to leave earlier than I had the last two mornings so I would have ample time to pick up coffee, since I kept forgetting to pick some up on the way home.

I had never imagined how busy my mother and sister were. Maybe I wouldn't need to find another place once I got a job, since I was practically alone most of the time.

My thoughts brought me to a stop on the stone walkway. Not, *once* I got a job … *if* I got a job. *If* I stayed. *If* I didn't get the part. The odd thing was that my thoughts hadn't even bothered me. For the first time since I could remember, the thought of not going back to New York didn't leave me feeling anxious.

Unlike that fateful morning twenty years ago when Markus and I had crossed the "just friends" line, and I'd begged Zayde to drive me to the train station. My mother had refused, stating she'd paid my way to spend the weekend home. My sister had said I was being selfish to leave over the holiday weekend. But Zayde had understood. He'd known I was lying, I was certain, when I'd told him I had an exam that I needed to study for and that I'd left my books in my dorm. My grandfather had known how emotional I was, and had driven me right to the station. As Markus had said, I'd left without a word to him, didn't explain why I couldn't stay, why I couldn't allow myself to see him again.

Pulling my mind back to the present, I hopped into my mother's old Taurus, excited to get going, excited to nail this part. Since I'd chased Markus away last night, and Raylene hadn't come downstairs, and Mom had been at the movies, I'd had nothing to do but run lines last night. I was now capable of reading the lines without the *sides*.

I turned the ignition, but all I heard was *click*. A dead *click*. An, *I'm dead and now you'll be late* click.

"No! God! No!" I tried again, but nothing. "Why?" I smashed my fingers over my eyes, then pulled my hands back, remembering I was wearing mascara. "Of all the days … of all the luck! How in the world could I have such bad luck?"

I lifted my phone and stared at it. I knew I didn't have a choice. My mother would be running the store, and Raylene ran a bank … There was only one person who could help me.

"Dammit!" I closed my eyes and slammed my head back against the headrest. I didn't have a choice. I picked up one of the fliers from the floor and dialed the number.

"Good morning, beautiful," Markus chirped.

How could he be so sweet after I was so … so … grouchy? But then a thought hit me. "Hey, how did you know it was me? I didn't give you my phone number."

"I asked Raylene for it a while ago. I just never got the nerve to call you."

"Oh …" I sighed, wondering what would have happened if he had contacted me. If we'd met in New York, would we have picked up where we left off when we were nineteen? Would he have stayed in New York if I'd asked him? Would I have followed him home if he'd asked me? Or, would I have rejected him and seen the dejected face I witnessed last night? I had no right to be so cruel. And I especially had no right to ask him for a favor after I'd treated him horribly. "Markus, I'm sorry —"

"It's okay, Laine. As I told you last night, this is my hang-up, not yours."

"Well, I am sorry about being a bitch last night, but that's not what I was apologizing for. I'm sorry because after acting that way, I have the nerve to ask you for a favor."

Markus's wonderful laughter floated through the phone. "You weren't being bitchy; you were being honest, and I can respect that. What do you need?"

My heart ached at his words. I had never deserved Markus. Not when we were kids, not now. "My mother's car won't start, and I'm supposedly first up today."

"I'll be right there." He hung up, and I dropped my head to the steering wheel as I'd done the previous evening.

Seriously, of all the days … Fate, the evil harpy she was, apparently didn't want me to land this role. Apparently, instead of being a good fairy godmother who wanted a happily-ever-after for me, she was evil and preferred to spend her days weaving schemes and cooking up mishaps and roadblocks for me to traverse. Like me, maybe the entity who oversaw my fate was interested in the theater, too, and thought that humor made for a good show.

Minutes into my self-loathing and ridiculous thoughts, an engine roared behind me. I whipped my head up to see Markus hop out of a Jeep, jumper cables strung over his shoulder.

"Pop the hood," he said as he strolled by, coming to a stop in front of the car.

I pulled on a latch, but nothing clicked.

Markus opened the driver's door and pushed my hand away. "That's the brake release. The trunk release is down here." Just a hint of soap interspersed with cinnamon wafted up from Markus. He always smelled so good. So clean. So …

The hood popped open with a *clunk*, and I jumped.

"You okay?" Markus asked as he patted my knee.

I licked my suddenly dry lips. "Yeah … Ummm … I'm just jumpy. Nervous about today."

He stared down at me for a brief second. "Of course. I can imagine. Let's see if we can get you on your way."

Markus moved to the hood of the car again and hefted up the cover, propping it open with a piece of metal. Zayde had taught me to drive when I was fifteen, but I knew nothing about cars. I'd never owned one. Right out of college I'd moved to New York.

"Give it a try," Markus called as he peeked at me around the hood.

I turned the key, and it continued to click.

"Are the lights and radio off?" he asked.

I inspected both. "Yep."

Markus walked back to the door. "The battery terminals are corroded, so I can't get a good connection. The car's been sitting too long." I looked up, wondering if he was making sexual innuendos again, but I didn't see humor in his eyes. "Come on," he said. "I'll take you so you won't be late."

"But ... don't you have to work at the store later today?" I was surprised he was willing to drive me, especially since he'd sounded as though he'd rather I didn't get the part last night.

"Not on Wednesdays."

I snatched my duffel bag off the seat. "Are you sure?" I inspected his clothes, which were even nicer than yesterday. Jeans again, but he had on a long-sleeve button-down plaid shirt over a black T-shirt. And not the old-fashioned red-and-black flannel plaid. The shirt was predominantly white and gray, with thin black lines. The stitching looked expensive. Then again, Markus had always dressed nicely. It looked as though he were dressed for a meeting.

"Of course, I'm sure." He walked with me to the passenger side of his vehicle, opening the door for me.

I turned to him before stepping up on the running board. "They told me I would go first today, but I've learned not to put much weight into statements made on the fly. It's the showbiz way. It might take all day again. If you drop me off, I can just catch a ride back via Uber."

"Ummm ... no. I'm not leaving you thirty miles from home. Besides," Markus winked, "I can write on my tablet wherever I am. Hop up before you're late."

Once again, Markus was proving how one-sided our friendship was. There had to be something I could do for him. What could I do for Markus to repay him? An idea popped into my mind and I shook it out. "Not that."

"What's that?" Markus asked as he hopped up into the Jeep on the driver's side.

"Nothing," I murmured. "Just practicing my lines."

He turned the ignition, and the engine roared to life. I glared at the unfaithful Taurus as we backed away from it, thinking, *See how easy that is, Taurus. Key turns, you start.* Now I was in the position of owing Markus. I didn't like owing people. Especially when paying him back meant more time around him, which meant more time to risk my heart. Something told me if I spent much more time with Markus, I might be stuck in Pittsburgh forever.

But as I'd thought a couple of times in the last few days, Pittsburgh might not be such a bad place to be stuck.

Hours passed as I waited in the room with a hundred or so other actors. Only this time, male and female, young and old actors, filled the room.

These were the final callbacks for all the parts, I assumed.

I stared around the room at my competition. About ten women fit what I thought were the minimum requirements to play the major lead. Then again, the script had a character who was about the same age as the lead, a literary agent. And then there was the main character's cousin, who was about ten years younger than she was.

What if they wanted me for a minor role? Would I be willing to put my life on hold — again — for a trivial role? I'd performed plenty of supporting roles over the years. They were nearly as much work, as I typically memorized all the lines so I'd know my cues. Money wasn't the issue either. I'd never cared about making a fortune. I just wanted one major role in my life. So no, if they only wanted me for a few scenes —

"Alaina Ackerman?" the monitor's voice broke me from my thoughts.

"Yes. I'm Alaina Ackerman." I hustled my way down the aisle of the few remaining hopefuls and followed the monitor into the next room, which led directly to the stage this time.

The lights were brighter than the first two times I'd stood here, making it hard to see, but I focused on the spot where Howard Edwards had sat the previous days. The seat was empty. Frantically, I squinted against the spotlights, searching every face. The best I could tell, Howard wasn't in any of the seats.

"Ms. Ackerman," a man called from somewhere below me.

To shield the onslaught of light, I lifted my hand to my brow. "Yes, sir?"

"Mr. Edwards has left for the day, and we already have your audition recorded, so we'll call you if we need you."

I bit down on my tongue. *Keep your mouth shut. Never open your mouth. Never respond with anything but thank you.* But I wanted to. I wanted to scream at him for making me waste three days of my life. Five days if I counted the practicing. Twenty years if I coupled him with every other CD who hadn't treated me as anything but an object.

But all I said was, "Thank you."

I scanned the wall behind me, looking for the exit through watery eyes. Why had they given me hope only to snatch it away again? I would have rather they'd been like the others: *Thanks. We'll call you.* Instead, they'd asked me back again and again. I'd thought I'd been fine with my lot. Thought I'd decided that I was through with auditions. But clearly, I'd been too pre-occupied with everything else going on around me — Joe's sudden departure; my employer going out of business; coming home; feelings about Markus — to grieve the loss of my career.

As I slammed through the glass exit doors, I dropped my *sides* into a trashcan. Markus had said to call him when I was finished, that he'd just be down the street, but I didn't want him to see me like this. I didn't want him to see that I was crying over something so stupid. After all, there were a lot worse things in the world. People were starving. People were dying. I was only losing a dream I'd chased after for twenty years. Surely that wasn't a good enough reason to want to drop down on the ground and cry my eyes out.

Wasn't a good reason that my heart felt like it was breaking in two.

But it was … Because just like someone who'd been cheated on, my career choice had cheated me. I'd given my career everything. Spent every day of the last twenty years starving myself. Spent thousands upon thousands of hours searching for casting calls, then wasted tens of thousands of hours practicing. Lived like a vagabond. Given up a chance to be a mother …

As soon as I was out of sight of the theater, I dropped down on a bench. I couldn't let Markus see me like this because I knew deep down I'd also given up a life with Markus, a life I knew I could have had with one word. I could have said *yes* twenty years ago. I could have chosen not to care what would have happened if we had sex. I hadn't been afraid of getting pregnant; I'd been on the pill. I knew Markus didn't have a disease because he'd never had a girlfriend. Asking if he had a condom had been the only way I knew to stop the inevitable. I'd said *no* when he hadn't been prepared to make love to me twenty years ago because I knew I hadn't been prepared to give up my career. Knew that going to the next level with Markus would have made it impossible to leave him.

Chapter 8 – The Cage

Long arms folded around me, but instead of jumping, I melted into the warmth of them. I knew these arms as though they were my own. And I could smell him.

"I'm so sorry, honey," Markus said as he slid onto the bench next to me.

I turned in his arms. "I just don't understand," I blubbered like a little kid. "Why call me back? Why did they tell me to come back if they didn't want to see me again, if Howard wasn't even going to be here?"

Markus tightened his arms around me, then smoothed his hands down the back of my head. "I don't know. It doesn't make sense. And believe me, I know how you feel. What it feels like to be rejected."

I pulled back just slightly and whispered into his neck, "I'm sorry. I didn't mean —"

He bent his head down, then wiped away my tears that were still falling. "Not by you, Laina, though that hurt too. By agents. I can't tell you how many times my query letters were rejected before I found an agent. It stings."

I hadn't thought about that. "Yeah … that would suck."

Markus pushed my hair back and kissed me on the forehead. His lips were warm and soft. It'd be so easy to forget about everything. To —

"Hey, let's go get those drinks," Markus said, breaking me out of my weak thoughts. "We'll drop off the Jeep, and go bar-crawling."

I laughed without meaning to. Leave it to Markus to have me laughing within seconds of bawling. "I haven't bar-crawled since I was in my twenties."

"Well, there are only a few good bars in Squirrel Hill, so it'll be a short crawl. Whaddya say?"

I sniffed. As always, just like when something didn't go right in high school, Markus would hug me and make me smile. We'd sit around and come up with creative names to call whomever we were mad at. I was sure I could come up with a few choice nicknames for Howard Edwards the Second. I sniffed. "Sure. Sounds like fun."

Markus parked behind the store. It was past five, so my mother would be long gone.

As soon as Markus unlocked the door, the pup started yipping.

"A new security system," I said.

"Yeah." Markus laughed. "That's what I told your mother."

"Oh? And how did she take the idea of a dog being in her shop?"

He shrugged. "Actually, she was pretty cool about it. She seemed to like him. As long as I make sure he's trained before I release him in the house or store, of course."

Markus leaned over a plastic gate he'd set up, which blocked the pup from having free rein of the store, but gave him room to run. "Let me take him outside real quick."

"Okay." I sniffed again, still trying to get a handle on myself after my crying jag. I felt so stupid, but Markus hadn't made me feel embarrassed at all. And he didn't seem happy about me failing, as I'd accused him of being last night. His eyes had genuinely been sad when he'd looked down at me. And his arms had been so warm. So comfortable. So … *Stop it, Alaina.*

"Good boy, Buddy," Markus said, and he and the pup came tromping back inside. "He's a smart one. He might be trained in no time."

I leaned down and scratched Buddy behind one ear. "What type of breed is he?"

Markus squatted down beside me. "Not sure. Mostly golden Lab, I think. But I can't tell what else. His nose is square, which reminds me of a boxer. It'd explain why he's so sweet and smart. I can't imagine a better mix than a Lab and boxer."

What kind of people *mix was Markus that made him so sweet?* I wondered. I'd never thought to ask. I tilted my head to look at the pup, but then pulled back when I bumped heads with Markus. "Yeah, I see it," I said, but really all I could think about was how close my legs were to Markus's … how close our mouths were …

"All right," Markus said as he picked up the pup and set him back behind the gate, "Let's go get you one of my sweatshirts."

"Me?"

"Yes, you. Do you think I'm going to give one of my prized Steelers or Pirates sweatshirts to Buddy? You know I can't be caught dead in Squirrel Hill with you wearing a

Yankees shirt. Maybe downtown, but not here. I have friends, you know."

I rolled my eyes. I thought about arguing, but the thought of stealing one of Markus's sweatshirts kept my mouth sealed.

Markus headed toward the stairs that led to his apartment, but I held back. "Aren't you coming?" he asked.

"Ummm …" I gulped, and then bit down on my lip. "I'm going to play with Buddy. Get him used to me in case I end up raising him."

Markus lifted his chin in what looked like a laugh, but then just said, "Okay. I'll be right back."

I petted Buddy, loving how soft his fur was. "You want to come home with me, boy?" He licked my hand and I continued to pet him. The thought of taking care of someone — something — other than myself was intriguing.

"Here you go." Markus tromped down the stairs. He handed me a Steelers sweatshirt that would be entirely too big.

"Thanks." I walked into the bathroom to change, but before I pulled it on, I lifted it to my face and inhaled. It smelled like Markus, Ivory soap and cinnamon. Maybe he had cinnamon in his apartment. I harrumphed to myself, then whispered softly to my reflection. "You don't know what you want, do you?"

"Well," Markus said as I stepped out of the bathroom, "I hate to sound cliché, especially since I'm a writer, but dannnnngggg, that shirt sure looks better on you than it does on me."

My cheeks burned. "What do you mean? It's practically falling to my knees."

"Exactly." He pulled softly on the V-neck, and I smacked his hand away. "What? Nothing I haven't seen before."

"Markus, if you don't behave …"

He lifted his chin, obviously doing his best not to smile. "You'll …?"

"Oh, let's just go."

Markus scooped up my hand and led me out the front door. "You hungry?" he asked as he locked up the shop. "It's kind of *divey*, but I thought we should get something to eat, and at The Cage we can eat and drink. The Penguins are playing, but since we're so early, we might even be able to get a great seat."

"That's exactly what I feel like doing, Markus. Heck, we don't even need to crawl anywhere else. We can party all night and practically crawl back to your place from there."

One side of Markus's face pulled up. "I'm game."

Markus hooked his arm around my waist, and it felt so natural I didn't even tease him. He certainly seemed more comfortable than the boy I'd known twenty years ago. Not that he hadn't been good in the truck … When he'd — my face burned again, so I immediately cut off my thoughts and focused on my feet.

Markus crossed the street at the end of the block, right beneath the Carnegie Library, which I planned to visit soon. It'd been too long since I'd caught up on my reading. Plus, I was certain I could find some books to study for the state teacher's exam.

He held open the red door, and I immediately bopped over to a booth, taking the one with my back to the door, as I knew from previous outings with Markus that he couldn't stand having his back to the door. Maybe because all the kids had picked on him in high school.

Even though I knew exactly what I was going to order, I snapped open the menu. Markus sat across from me and opened his, even though I knew exactly what he would order, too.

"By the way," I said, peeking over my menu at Markus, "I plan to gain twenty pounds."

Markus set down his menu and met my eyes. "Well, since we're not dating, I feel as though I can ask a question. Am I supposed to say, 'Good! You need to gain weight.' Or, 'Why? You look great exactly the way you are.'?"

I shrugged. "Neither. I was just letting you know so you wouldn't start worrying about me when I start to put on weight."

He tilted his head just slightly. "Should I be worried?"

"Nope. I've been on a diet since I was fourteen, and I told myself if I didn't get this part I was going to finally eat."

Markus smiled. "Works for me. As long as you're happy, I'm happy."

I sighed inwardly at his perfect answer, but tried to focus on my task at hand, enjoying my meal. Yes, I was still going to order a salad, but I was going to order it *Pittsburgh style*. Not once in my life had I been able to try the delicious notion of adding sizzling hot French fries, grilled chicken, and gobs of shredded cheddar cheese to a perfectly healthy salad. But tonight that would all change.

"Ready to order?" asked a dark-haired woman dressed in a plain T-shirt and jeans, no uniform. No, *Hello*. No, *How are you?* No, *Have you been here before?* Like Markus had said, The Cage was *divey*, but it was Squirrel Hill *divey*, and that's how we locals liked it. No pretenses. If you were new, it was your job to make friends, not the locals' job to introduce you.

I looked up at the woman and smiled. "I'll take the grilled chicken salad, Pittsburgh style, with extra cheese and ranch dressing."

"Make that two," Markus said, surprising me, as he normally always ordered a cheesesteak with a salad, no fries. Maybe he wanted to join me on my quest of gaining weight and raising my cholesterol.

"And to drink?" the woman asked.

"Oh, right. Ummm ..." I did a mental calculation of the calories in hard cider versus wine, nearly double. It was hard not to think about calories when you'd been counting them daily for two decades. Regardless, I said, "I'll have whatever hard cider you have."

Markus smiled and said, "Make that two," again.

I pushed his hands, which were resting in front of him in a low clasp, not a steeple, but more like he was holding one of his hands up with the other. "You planning to join me in my downward spiral?"

He grabbed my hand in his and lowered both our hands to the table. "Why stop now? I always did whatever crazy thing you wanted to do when we were kids. So, what exactly did Howard the Coward do?"

"And on with the name calling ... You remembered." A familiar warmth rushed through me for no reason.

"Of course." Markus smiled. "So, what happened? You need me to beat him up?"

"As if ... Since when did you start offering to beat up my enemies?"

"You have no idea what I did in high school to protect your honor." Confused, I narrowed my eyes, but Markus waved off my question. "What happened, Laina? A third callback is good, right?"

"Yes ... usually. It wasn't what Howard *Schmoward*," the best I could come up with on short notice, "did, it's what he didn't do. As I told you before, the first two days Howard just stood and left, demanding that callbacks be back at ten a.m. But then today, after they left me sitting in that room for hours, he just didn't show. Maybe they were waiting for him. I don't know. Anyway, the CD just said, 'We already have your audition recorded, so we'll call you if we need you.' Which means they've already made a decision."

Markus squeezed my hands. "I'm sorry, Laina. I really am."

I didn't really want to talk about the audition. Before I could change the subject, though, the waitress brought us two bottles of Angry Orchard. No glass, of course, which I was used to at The Cage; a bartender once mentioned that they only had so many glasses and not enough room to keep them chilled.

Markus pulled back his hands and lifted his bottle. "To rejections, may we only learn from them, and not want to rip up our manuscripts or give up over them."

I lifted my bottle to his but then shook my head. "I have to give up, Markus. I'm too old."

Markus lowered his head and stared me in the eyes. "You look amazing, Laina, better than ninety percent of women who are half your age."

"You're biased, Markus."

He lifted one eyebrow and shrugged. "Maybe. Maybe not."

"Markus," I paused, taking another sip, "Why haven't you gotten married?"

He took another sip, then licked his lips. "It appears you don't keep as good of tabs on me as I've kept on you. I'm not sure how I feel about that."

"What do you mean?"

"I *was* married, Laina. For ten years."

"Oh. I didn't —" I was surprised I hadn't heard about Markus getting married. Then again, why would my mother tell me something that wouldn't further the chance of me coming home or giving her grandkids? But I was even more surprised by the rush of heat that soared through my heart. Not a tickle, but red-hot heat — anger or jealousy — something I rarely felt. I pushed the emotions aside the best I could. "What happened?"

He shrugged again. "It just didn't work out. We drifted apart, then one day she asked me for a divorce. I'll admit, I was surprised. It wasn't as though we fought. She just wanted more, and I guess I've always been simpler. That's when I quit working for my father and went back to school. I knew what I'd always wanted, but had been too afraid to go after." He paused and looked up at me, his green eyes shiny. "Well, one of my dreams anyway —"

The waitress brought our meals, halting his words. Perfect timing.

"Ooh … this looks so good." I unwrapped the napkin from around my silverware, then drizzled ranch all over the salad. I speared a perfect bite of fries, chicken, cheese, lettuce, and tomato. I bit down and then moaned as the combination of hot and cold, sweet and salty lit up my taste buds. I stabbed my fork down again, scooping up as much as I could at once before the fries got cold and the salad got warm.

A few bites in, I stopped eating, noticing that Markus hadn't moved. "Don't stop," he said. "I like watching you be happy."

I reached for the cider and downed the bottle and then sat back. "Oh, my. I'm very happy right now."

Markus downed his cider, then caught the waitress's eye as she started to dart past us. He motioned to our empty bottles, and she nodded.

"So," I started before he could continue, "no kids?"

"She didn't want any. One of our major differences. She wanted us to take over my parents' business and didn't want to be tied down by children." He shook his head. "Her words. Of course, my parents were never home when I was a kid, so I guess I understand. But they still loved me, and I had you guys."

The waitress dropped off two more bottles, and I reached for one immediately, downing the ice-cold cider almost completely. I'd consider the cider a 180-calorie dessert, then switch to drinking wine the rest of the night.

"Thirsty?" Markus laughed.

"Yes, but no more cider. Let's switch to wine. Cider is too filling." I pushed the salad away, then stood. "I'm done with the food, too. I'll be right back."

"White or red?"

My mental calculator went off again. Cabernet has fewer calories, but Chardonnay has less carbs. Remembering I didn't care, though, I said, "Whatever you want."

He nodded, then signaled the waitress before I turned and headed off to the washroom.

When I came back, Markus slid out of the booth, motioning for me to sit on his side of the table. I obeyed, and he slid in next to me.

A wave of heat surged up my back and neck, so I pulled my hair off my neck, twisted it, and laid it on my shoulder. I reached for the glass of white wine in front of me.

Markus turned to me and just the look in his eyes made the heat rush down the front of my body. "Are you really giving up, Laina?"

I averted my eyes, shutting off my view of him. How had I not noticed how good-looking Markus was? Other than filling out, he looked exactly as he had in high school.

He touched my cheek. "Look at me, Laina."

I pulled my eyes away from the scarred table, looking up at him.

"You've done well, right? You've made a living. Why would you quit if it's what you love?"

What I love? "Because ..." I raised my hand to my face and rubbed my head, cutting off my view of him again.

Markus reached for my hand and held it in his lap. "Because?"

I wanted to tell him the truth. I wanted to say, *Because I'm falling in love with you, and I know I can't have both* ... Not when an acting career would take me back to New York or Hollywood. But I couldn't tell him that I was falling in love. Not until I knew for sure what I wanted, what I was feeling. Markus stared at me as if he'd read my mind again, as if it'd break his heart if I left again, so I just told him the only truth I knew for certain. "I don't know."

Markus leaned forward, his lips inches from mine. I started to shut my eyes, to open my mouth, to accept him, but my phone buzzed.

I shook my head. "Sorry. I don't think to turn off my phone because I rarely get calls. It might be Mom."

I pulled the phone out of the side pocket of my purse and read the text from Joe. *Where are you, Alaina? Where are all your things?*

Confused, I stared at the text. Was Joe back at the apartment? Then I realized, he'd said they were flying him out. He hadn't said that he was staying. He'd only taken one suitcase with him.

"Do you need to answer that?" Markus asked.

Nervous at once, I rubbed my hand over my mouth, realizing that Markus had been able to read the text. Not that I'd hidden it from him. I had assumed it was from Mom. "Ummm ... maybe just to let him know I'm alive."

"You didn't tell him you were going home?"

"It was sort of an on-the-fly decision. I just packed up and left so I wouldn't miss the four o'clock train."

All I could hope was that Markus wouldn't get offended, because really, it would be wrong for me not to answer Joe. I typed out a quick: *I'm in Pittsburgh. I'll explain later.*

Markus turned so his back was up against the booth again. He ran his hands up the sides of his nose, past the area between his eyebrows, across his forehead, and then rubbed his temples.

I held up the phone so he could see what I was doing, then clicked off the ringer. "Markus …"

He turned just his head to me. "Yes?"

"I don't know what you want me to say."

He released a puff of air, which sounded like a laugh, but not his normal happy laugh. He sounded frustrated, and Markus never sounded frustrated. "I don't *want* you to say anything, Alaina. I want you to *want* to say something." He turned to me. "I want you to *want* to say you're sorry. I want you to *want* to be with me."

My heart exploded into a vicious rhythm. "Markus … I just —"

He turned to me, his face moving to mine before I could react. Instead of kissing me, as it seemed he intended, he said, "Let's go." Markus pulled out his wallet, fishing through the bills until he found a fifty. He motioned to the waitress again, then dropped the fifty on the table.

He took my hand and gently coaxed me out of the booth. He reached for my coat on the hook and held it while I shrugged into it.

Once again, he took my hand in his. Not that I had a choice, it seemed, but I let him trail me out the door. Of course, I had a choice. I could demand that he let go of my hand, but I didn't want to. I wanted to talk to him. And he was right. We needed to be in private for this conversation.

At least I'd only had two glasses of cider, which wasn't nearly as strong as wine.

Without a word, Markus wrapped his arm around my waist and escorted me back the way we'd come. Across the street and then back to the shop. Instead of going in through the front door of the shop, he walked down the alley to the rear of the store.

Markus lifted his fingers to his lips. "If we go through the store, Buddy will wake up, and he needs his sleep."

I resisted smiling, imagining for just a second that Buddy was our kid.

Markus directed me up the black iron stairs that led to the apartment above the shop, then followed closely behind me.

When he opened the door and turned on the light, I was surprised to see how open and airy the small apartment was. Nothing like the dark flat where my sister and I had done our homework while Mom had worked downstairs.

The floors had a high polish on them, and the kitchen had all black cabinets and chrome appliances with lights beneath the cabinets that cast light on the granite countertops. Markus led me to the opposite side of the apartment, the living area. The area was tidy, but full. Every inch of wall space consisted of artwork or shelves decorated with books. The little floor space there was held a wide walnut desk with nothing but a laptop perched on top, a leather sofa and coffee table the color of dark chocolate, and more bookshelves, stuffed with more books. Maybe that was why my mother had always loved Markus. It appeared he read as much as she did.

Without a word, Markus took my hand and coaxed me to the couch. "What was it you wanted to say, Laina?"

I smiled without meaning to. "I wanted to tell you I'm sorry ..."

"For?" he pressed.

"Everything …"

He shook his head. "Too broad."

I stared up at his stern face. "For not calling you back after I took advantage of you when you were nineteen."

"That's a start." A small smile lifted one corner of his mouth. "But you didn't take advantage of me." He released a soft breath while he shook his head. "I knew what I wanted. Why do you think I brought two bottles of wine? I wasn't as innocent as you always assumed I was."

"You weren't?"

"Nope." He lifted my hand and placed it around his neck and then pulled my other hand around his waist.

Markus moved his large hand around my waist and tugged me forward, stopping within inches of my lips. "Alaina Ackerman, I'll forgive you for not calling me back twenty years ago and for not noticing how much I wanted you when we were teenagers if you'd simply *want* to kiss me right now."

My heart rate sped up again and my mouth quirked up on both ends. I wasn't sure if I wanted to laugh or cry. The one thing I knew, though, was that I wanted to kiss Markus Klein. I used my hand that he'd placed behind his neck and pulled him forward.

That was all the invitation he needed. In a flash, Markus scooped me up in his arms without breaking our kiss and carried me into the only other large room in the apartment. He didn't flick on a switch, but the light from the streetlamps filtered through the blinds, casting white streaks across the room, the bed, and even Markus. The slices of white made his square chin look even stronger. In the striped light, he looked almost feral, not the innocent teenager who played a part in my sexual fantasies night after night.

A hunger rose up inside of me that I hadn't felt in twenty years. He lowered me to the bed, but held his arm behind my back so I was sitting, then sat down beside me.

Markus swept my hair off my shoulder, then touched his lips to my neck. "I don't want you to leave again, Alaina. I want you to stay here. With me."

What was he asking me? Technically, we'd only been seeing each other for three days. I had said that I wouldn't leave. That I would stay in Pittsburgh. But his asking me to stay — with him — was something different.

As much as I wanted to fight his words, I turned to his kiss. If we were kissing, we couldn't talk about plans, which meant neither of us would lie.

His mouth enveloped mine, his tongue touching mine, making me remember. He wanted me to remember. To remember him. To remember one hot night when we were too young to know what we wanted. After all, I'd thought I wanted to be a star. He'd thought he wanted to take over his father's million-dollar company.

We were both wrong. We'd wanted each other. Then. Now. But then again, maybe I'd been smart to leave. If I'd stayed with Markus in Pittsburgh twenty years ago, I would have probably resented him. And he probably would have continued to work for his father to provide for our kids and me. And we would have both been miserable.

My hand moved to the hem of his sweatshirt, and I attempted to pull it up.

Markus moved his hands over mine, effectively stopping me. "Not yet. Just stay with me. I don't know if I'm strong enough to have all of you only to lose you again." His mouth moved to mine again as he scooted us both up in the bed. He moved me to my back and hovered over me. His lips moved from my mouth to my chin, then down my neck, stopping and nibbling along the way.

He pulled the neckline of the shirt low enough to expose the swell of my breasts as he continued his kisses downward. His mouth stopped its progression as he pulled back. "You know, you slapped my hand away a few hours ago for just peeking."

I threw my head back. "What can I say, you're like a drug. Peer pressure, you know?"

Markus fell on his side and pulled me up alongside him, his arms tightening around me. He kissed the top of my head. "I love you, Alaina. I've always loved you."

I lifted my head to look at Markus. "I love you too, Markus."

"But?" he said softly.

"No *but*. I do love you. I've always loved you, too."

He smoothed my hair from my face. "Just not in the same way?"

"Markus," I closed my eyes again to assemble my thoughts, "Yes, in the same way. I just need a little bit of time to sort out my life."

He pressed his lips to my forehead for a few seconds, then pulled back to look at me. "As long as you stay here and sort out your life, I'll wait for you forever."

"And if I decide not to give up on acting, to move back to New York?" I hedged.

He sighed and lowered his forehead to mine. "I don't know."

At least Markus was honest, and that's all I could ask. I nestled my head beneath his chin and closed my eyes. Markus did feel like home. A home I never wanted to leave. But I had to know for sure. It wouldn't be right to hurt Markus — again.

Chapter 9 – Puppies and Babies, Oh My!

The sound of barking woke me up, and then toenails tapping on the wood floor grew louder with each passing second. I opened my eyes, but bright streaks of sunshine caused me to shut them again.

"Is that better?" I heard Markus's silky voice.

With my arm over my face, I chanced opening one eye, the one farthest away from the bright white rays.

Only a few streams of light filtered through, so I opened both my eyes and searched for Markus. It was still too bright.

Markus set something on the nightstand and then sat down next to me. "Are you always this confused in the morning?"

"Yeah. I tend to sleep in." I breathed in and out, attempting to hide a yawn as I nestled myself deeper into the pillow. It smelled so good. Like Markus. "What time is it?"

"Ten."

"Oh!" I sat up. "Oh, no! Mom's going to be worried." I'd planned to get up in the middle of the night and sneak home. I never slept through the night. But I'd felt so warm and safe in Markus's arms.

"Belinda's downstairs, and she's fine. She knew you were with me all day, remember? I drove you to the audition when the Taurus went kaput."

I stifled another yawn. "That's right." It seemed longer than a day ago that I was crying about losing a role again.

Markus jutted his chin to the nightstand. "I brought coffee."

"Oh. Thank you!" I reached for the cup. "God, you're wonderful."

Markus laughed. "I can cook and wash dishes, too."

I squinted at him over the cup as I inhaled the dark roasted goodness. We had the same taste in coffee. "Mmmm."

"Drink. I have to go to work."

"Work?" I set down the cup. "I thought you only worked in the afternoons."

Markus leaned over me and kissed my forehead. "Two thousand words. As soon as I knock out two thousand words, I'm free."

"Oh … How long does that take, and free to do what?"

"A few hours, then my brain typically turns off. I was thinking a walk in Frick Park would be fun, remind you how beautiful it is here, and give Buddy some exercise, and then maybe we could get ice cream at Waffallonia."

"Oh … so you're going to assist me in gaining twenty pounds, are you?"

"If that's what you want." He turned to leave.

"Ummm, Markus?"

He stopped in the doorway, and I couldn't help but notice that he looked just as good in gray sweatpants and a white T-shirt as he had in designer jeans.

"I need to take a shower."

"Help yourself." He pointed to the white door across from me. "There're spare toothbrushes beneath the cabinet. I use an electric toothbrush, but every six months I get a free toothbrush from the dentist, and I haven't had company in a while, so you have your pick."

I gazed up at him, surprised by his words, wondering how many toothbrushes were beneath the sink. "Clothes?"

"Help yourself to anything in my closet."

I sighed, then decided to ask for something I was sure he wouldn't have. "Makeup?"

"You got me there." He laughed. "But you don't need any. I've seen you worse."

I snatched a pillow from behind me and threw it at him. "I should just go home."

Markus caught the pillow up in mid-air. "Okay. But your mother is downstairs. You can leave out the back steps, but you know how Belinda seems to have a sixth sense. Good luck sneaking past her."

My mouth dropped open. "What did you tell her?"

"I didn't tell her anything. She asked if you stayed here, and I said yes. End of discussion."

"She didn't ask anything else?"

Markus shook his head. "Why would she? She knew you were with me. But I'm sure she has questions for you."

True … My mother had never concerned herself with my hanging out with Markus. She trusted him completely, even when we were in high school. But Markus was right, she was sure to have questions for me, questions I'd have no idea how to answer, since I didn't know the answers myself. I could walk home, as I'd planned to do last night; the house was only two streets away.

Markus, seemingly reading the look on my face, reached into his pocket and tossed a set of car keys on the bed. "Just be back by two, okay?"

I smiled up at him. "Sure."

Buddy tugged on the makeshift leash Markus had made from Velcro and a cord from my mother's shop. When tugging didn't enable him to chase the birds and children, though, he would reach his head around and try to bite the line.

Markus didn't fuss or seem to get irritated, though. He'd simply discipline Buddy softly, and then start walking again the moment Buddy behaved. Buddy seemed way too young to teach, and yet he was learning. Markus would make a great father, I realized, and then tried to shake the image of Markus bouncing a baby on his knee.

What was I thinking? Both Markus and I were close to turning the big Four-O. Where exactly would we find a child to bounce on his knee?

"Have you ever thought of being a *Big Brother*, Markus?" I suddenly asked, since I couldn't shake the dozens of images of Markus holding a baby that bombarded my brain.

"My parents are rather old to have children, Laina," he said through a chuckle.

"You know what I mean." I playfully shoved him off the sidewalk, and Buddy, sensing a chance to escape the concrete, bolted into the grass, entangling his leash with Markus's legs.

Markus knelt to disentangle Buddy, then reached up and grabbed my hand and tugged me down on top of him. "If you don't behave, I'll hold you down and let Buddy give you kisses all over your face, and Lord only knows what he's put his mouth and tongue into today."

Knowing one way to apologize and distract Markus, I extended my head to reach his mouth and kissed him. Not a long kiss; we were in a public park, after all. But a light peck to distract him.

Markus closed his eyes and kissed me back deeper than I expected, then rolled me to my side and pulled away from my lips. "I wish …"

Yip! Yip! Yip! Buddy tugged on his leash, struggling to reach a small child that was lumbering toward us.

An out-of-breath woman caught up to the little boy. "Sorry. We just read a book, and the dog looked exactly like your pup."

Markus got to his feet and offered me his hand. "It's no problem." He squatted down and took hold of Buddy so he couldn't jump on the toddler. "You can pet him. Just be careful. He's a baby."

The curly blond-haired toddler inched his way closer. "Ba … by?"

"He's a puppy, which is a baby dog, so yes."

The little boy squeezed his hand open and closed on Buddy's head, so Markus took the little boy's hand and showed him how to pet the pup.

"Thank you," the woman said, sounding embarrassed. "We keep wondering if it's time to get him a puppy, but we don't want him to terrorize it."

They could adopt Buddy, I realized, but then a pang of regret hit my stomach. I didn't want anyone to have Buddy but me and — or Markus, I corrected my thoughts.

"That's smart," Markus answered the woman, then looked down at the toddler who was ever so gently trying to pet Buddy, and Buddy didn't seem to be bothered at all, as some dogs were by young children. "It looks like he's close."

The woman stooped down and scooped up her child. "We'll talk to Daddy, okay?"

"O-tay," the little boy answered her with a sniff.

"Say bye to the nice doggie," his mother said.

The little boy opened and closed his hand. "Bye, doggie."

Markus raised Buddy's paw and waved.

You're killing me! I wanted to scream. Puppies and babies. Mommies and Daddies. Markus with a puppy and a baby. All the things I'd never have.

When the woman disappeared over the hill, Markus turned to me, "Ready for ice cream?"

"Yes!" Not that an ice cream parlor would be any better, but we needed to get out of here before I started humming the wedding march or lullabies.

After we'd gorged ourselves on fresh homemade sugar waffles topped with cinnamon ice cream, Markus drove me back to my house, but didn't turn off the ignition when he pulled into the driveway.

Not wanting the day to be over, I turned to him. "Wanna come inside?"

"Sure."

It felt like we were in high school again. Was it really possible to start over? To get a second chance? We weren't teenagers, but we were still just a boy and a girl who'd taken the wrong path at one point. Next to Markus, I felt young again. I felt like I could really start over.

Markus and Buddy followed me into the mudroom.

Even though I was stuffed, my mouth watered as soon as I stepped inside the kitchen. "Yum." I turned to Markus.

"It smells like Mom made your favorite." I walked over to the crockpot. I wanted to lift up the lid, to release all the steam and steal a chunk of chicken that I knew would be tender and flavorful, but she'd smack my butt with the towel if she caught me.

Markus inhaled deeply, as did Buddy. "Chicken and dumplings and it's not even my birthday. She must need me to pull an extra shift." Markus wrapped his arm around my waist and pulled me toward him. "I was going to take you out … to a real meal, but I guess …"

I stared up at Markus. I'd forgotten how tall he was until I was wearing flats and standing right next to him. "A home-cooked meal sounds good. Maybe we can do something later?"

He kissed my forehead and then my cheek. "What did you have in mind?"

"Anything good showing at the Manor?"

"It wouldn't matter if there was, I wouldn't be able to concentrate anyway."

I sighed. "More honesty. I'm not used to that."

"I told you, Laina. I'm not going to make the same mistake I made twenty years ago by not telling you exactly how I feel."

"Okay … Well, maybe we'll just watch something on Netflix, then. I haven't binge-watched any series lately. You up for that?"

"Absolutely, I'm up for binge-watching, like we used to watch *Friends* episodes back-to-back, then flip to another channel and watch two more." Buddy wound his way around our legs. "I guess Buddy wants to stay, too, or maybe he just likes seeing us pressed together."

"Ahem!" A clearing of a throat had both of us wobbling as Markus struggled to unwind the leash along with Buddy from around our legs.

My mother walked past us. "I would have thought that the two of you got enough of that last night."

Markus finally got Buddy loose. "Sorry, Belinda. New pup still needs lots of training."

My mother flashed a smile, then winked at Markus. "No calls from his owners, huh?" She bent down, and Buddy leapt toward her. Apparently anything or anyone below knee-level was open territory. "You are a cute fellow, aren't you? Who could possibly let a boy as good as you go? Sweet, loving, and smart are hard to find in one package."

I cocked my head at Markus, then stared down at my mother. "I'm going to go get cleaned up. You know your way around, Markus."

Markus smiled at me innocently, but I wasn't buying it. The two of them were in cahoots. "I do. I'll take the pup outside again. Make sure there are no accidents inside. I don't want him to wear out our welcome." He marched off to the back door, and I flashed my mother a glare.

My mother held up her hands. "What did I do?"

"Nothing." I charged up the stairs. I wasn't sure why it bothered me. I'd told myself I wanted to stay in Pittsburgh. But when they ganged up on me it brought out my inner child, and I immediately wanted to buck authority. I wasn't perfect Raylene, who never got in trouble.

Speaking of Raylene … Where was she? Why had it felt like she'd avoided me all week? I'd been wanting to ask what happened between her and Russell, since they'd seemed perfect for each other. Maybe she thought Mom was paying more attention to me since I was home, which wasn't the case at all. I'd barely seen either of them. Only Markus seemed to be available every spare minute. Was Markus normally here? I wondered.

What if? No … It couldn't be. I pushed the idea out of my head and headed to Raylene's room. I needed something to wear.

One good thing about having a sister in the house was that it doubled my clothing supply. We'd always swapped clothes, so I was sure she wouldn't mind if I borrowed something. I'd wash clothes in the morning.

It was after six, but I hadn't seen Raylene, so I assumed she was still at work. It was hard to tell when she was home, since she got the spare space in the garage because her car was new. I wasn't sure if any amount of money was worth working as hard as my sister worked.

To be polite, I still knocked on the door as I opened it. "Ray?" I peeked in and was surprised to see that she was home. But she was in bed. I walked to her bed, which still had the white eyelet comforter she'd had since high school. I'd chosen a purple set. "Ray? You okay?" Apparently, her breakup with Russell was weighing on her hard, which was understandable since they'd been together so long. But Raylene had never let anything bring her down, even a breakup; she'd always taken everything "like a champ," as Zayde would have said. Raylene had always been Zayde's strong girl, the clever one, the smart one … I'd been the emotional one.

Raylene opened her eyes. "Oh, hey, Lain. Yeah. Just tired. Thought I'd catch a nap before dinner."

"Oh … I could come back. It's not important."

She yawned. "No, no it's okay. I'm up. What do you need?"

"I was wondering … could I borrow something to wear? I haven't had a chance to wash clothes."

Raylene pushed the blanket back and sat up. "Sure. Whatever you want." A couple seconds later, she walked past her closet into the bathroom.

"Mom made chicken and dumplings," I said, just for something to say.

"I smell it," Raylene said. "Is Markus here?"

"Yeah …" I couldn't tell if that upset her or not. She hadn't seemed upset the other night when he was here. And Markus hadn't acted strange around her either. Maybe Markus was as oblivious to Raylene, as I'd been to him in high school. Three years seemed like a lot in high school, but thirty-nine and forty-two were nothing but two numbers of middle-aged people.

Since Markus lived alone — with two extra toothbrushes beneath his sink — my mother had probably been inviting him to dinner on a regular basis. I was sure that the two extra toothbrushes didn't mean that he hadn't dated in a year, but based on the way he'd mentioned them, I took it to mean that he hadn't had overnight guests. If Markus had been spending a lot of time at the house, it was possible that Raylene —

"What did you decide to wear?" Raylene asked, making me jump.

"Sorry …" I laughed. "I don't know why I jumped. Just thinking, I guess. I don't know what to choose; they're all so nice. I just need something simple." All of my sister's clothes were expensive-looking. Her closet was like a female version of Joe's closet with all its professional button-down shirts and jackets.

"Here," Raylene reached up on a shelf and pulled down a pair of jeans, "You'll like these. They used to be my favorite." She slid a few hangers aside, then tugged down a pink Steelers sweatshirt. "You look good in pink. Markus will like that."

"Ummm …"

She furrowed her brow. "Oh, come on. You think I didn't notice that you didn't come home last night?"

I shook my head, worried that maybe I was wrong, maybe she *was* irritated that I'd come home. "Nothing happened. We just had a few drinks and talked."

"Why on earth not?" Raylene planted her hands on her hips. "Markus is crazy about you. He's always been crazy about you. If you're staying in Pittsburgh, why wouldn't you want to see where it might lead?"

I nodded, but stared my sister deep in the eyes. She never was a good liar. I was the one who could stretch the truth. "Would you like that, Ray? If I stayed … if something became of Markus and me?"

Raylene stepped forward and wrapped her arms around me. "I would love it if you came home, Lain. Mom needs you. Markus needs you. I need you."

I leaned back, wanting to assess her eyes. She'd hidden her eyes by hugging me, so I couldn't tell, when she'd breathed those words, if she'd been completely honest, but she'd sounded sincere.

I could try a more straightforward approach. "Do you like Markus?"

She huffed out a laugh, and her eyes stayed on mine this time. "Of course I like Markus. What's not to like? I think you'd really be happy with him."

I sighed. "Yeah … I think so, too."

"But …"

I laughed. "Why does everyone think there's a *but* when I say something?"

"Because I know there's a *but*. This is your life, Laina. You need to make sure, whatever you do, that you're happy. We only have one lifetime, so it's important that we make the most of it."

I exhaled a long breath. "Yeah, and half of mine is already gone. I don't want to mess up the next half, but I also hate to think that I wasted the first half."

Raylene rested her cool hand against my cheek. "Just take it day by day. You'll know what to do. Start by getting dressed so we can go eat."

I lifted the clothes in my hands. "Thanks! I'll be right down."

I walked down a flight of steps to my room, hoping that Raylene was being honest with me, since the last thing I wanted was to hurt her. I just couldn't shake the feeling that she wasn't happy that I was home, maybe the reason I hadn't seen her for more than a few minutes at a time since I'd arrived.

Chapter 10 – Scandal or Hype

Stuffed from the three helpings of chicken and dumplings I'd eaten, I pulled a pillow on my lap. I was glad Raylene had given me a sweatshirt to wear, since I felt as if my belly might explode.

It appeared that gaining twenty pounds wasn't going to be a difficult task at home, especially since I wasn't burning any calories by working.

Markus flipped through the stations while I searched the menu on the Netflix app on my phone. Every time I mentioned a thriller, he'd say "too scary for Buddy." Then he'd suggest a romantic comedy.

"Wait!" I screeched as he surfed by a station. I was positive I'd heard the announcer mention the film I'd auditioned for.

"What?" Markus asked.

"Go back a notch … local station. News reporter, I think."

Markus flicked back a channel, then another, pausing and waiting for my reaction.

Raylene walked in and sat on the recliner where Zayde had always sat. She'd changed into an extra-large sweatshirt and sweatpants; the worn gray fabric literally hung off her.

Mom set down a large stainless bowl filled to the brim with popcorn. "What did you decide to watch — ?"

"There!" I shouted. "Stop!" The top right corner of the screen indicated a live feed.

The cameraman focused on a man standing next to red velvet-covered ropes outside one of the swanky restaurants inside one of the equally posh hotels in downtown Pittsburgh, then panned the camera toward a pearl-white Audi convertible, one of those tri-colored paint jobs that raised the price of even expensive cars another thousand dollars. Dressed in a black tux, Howard Edwards walked around the front of the car just as a valet started to open the passenger door for someone.

Hundreds of flashes ensued. "Oh ..." Jana Embers stepped out of the car but then stumbled from the onslaught of flashing bright lights.

Howard steadied her by wrapping his arm around her, then turned her away from the paparazzi.

"Mr. Edwards," the reporter who'd been waiting for their arrival called after them, "my sources tell me that Jana will be playing the starring role in *You Don't Need a Man*. Is that true?"

Howard peeked down at Jana Embers.

The camera caught her profile as she looked up at him, her mouth turning down as though she were confused.

Howard said something the camera didn't pick up, and Jana shrugged.

Then, Howard turned to the reporter, his arm still wrapped around Jana, and flashed his million-dollar smile, the one that had earned him a spot on Hollywood's most-eligible-bachelor list nearly every year. "As capable as Ms. Embers is to be cast in the movie, that rumor is not true."

A female reporter stepped into the camera shot and motioned her hand toward Howard's arm around Jana's waist. "Any chance of other leading roles?"

Howard pulled Jana closer, then turned her toward him, immediately locking his lips with hers.

"Oh …" Mom and I cooed at the same time, and I was pretty sure my heart cranked up a notch as if Howard had kissed me instead of Jana. I'd been right that Howard's head wasn't in the game. His sights had been on the author.

Raylene released a soft, dare I say, disbelieving chuckle. I couldn't put my finger on why her laugh didn't sound right. I stared at my sister, waiting for her to make eye contact with me and explain, but she covered her mouth with her hand as though she were as shocked as Mom and I were.

"What's the big deal?" Markus asked. "Why do women get all googly-eyed over him? He grew up in the same town as all of us."

"He did?" I asked, turning toward Markus.

"Yeah. He grew up in Squirrel Hill, went to the same high school as you and I did. Well, not the same year." Markus looked at Raylene. "He would have been within a few years of your class, though, Ray. Did you know him?"

Raylene shrugged. "He's a few years older than I am."

I stared back and forth at both of them. "You guys know Howard Edwards the Second and you didn't think to tell me when I was auditioning for his movie. Having an 'in' — no matter how small — helps."

Markus raised his hands. "I don't *know* him. I know *of* him. My father knew his father back in the day." Markus paused. "You know, come to think of it, maybe my father does know Howard too. I seem to remember a couple years back that some huge Hollywood producer was looking for a great deal in Mount Washington. I just never put the two together."

I shoved him on the shoulder. "Markus! I can't believe ... Ugh!"

Irritated, I turned my head back to the TV when Howard started speaking again.

"I can tell you one thing," Howard said, "if Jana were my woman, I'd never have her wondering if she needed a man." He turned away, his arm still latched around Jana's waist, and headed for the front doors of the hotel.

I laughed at his statement as I realized the scene had probably been a publicity stunt, since his words nearly matched the title of the movie. Even Jana auditioning for the role in her own movie had probably been set up to cause people like the gossiping actors who'd been outside the theater to spread the info to the media.

A pang of dejection hit me as I realized that, based on the cordoned-off area and the reporters waiting, it wasn't a coincidence they'd run into Howard and Jana. No, Howard had been escorting Jana to a party, a casting party announcing the leads.

Oh, well ... that was it then. My career as an actress was finally over. Of course, I'd already known that, the reason I'd had my mental breakdown after the CD had dismissed me. Sure, I could continue to accept small roles and commercials. I'd made a decent living for the last twenty years. But I didn't want that. I needed to settle down. And I couldn't settle down if I was always running from one audition to the next. And Raylene had said that Mom needed me, that she needed me.

I glanced up to ask Raylene about her reaction to seeing Howard, since based on her comment about him being a few years older than her told me she did, in fact, know that Howard went to the same high school. But she was gone.

"Where did Ray go?" I asked my mother.

"Ray gets up early in the morning, so she normally goes to bed early."

"Oh …" I said, then snatched the remote out of Markus's hands. "Give me that. You'll surf all night."

Markus leaned back into the corner of the sofa and pulled me against him. "Pick whatever you want."

My insides warmed immediately. This felt right. Markus felt right.

Tomorrow I'd figure out how to apply for my teacher's certification. After all, what was left for me in New York now that Joe had left and I'd decided to retire from auditioning?

Chapter 11 – Proposals

Monday morning. A new week, a new beginning. Over the weekend, since Markus was working on a deadline, he'd said, and Mom and Raylene had been out of sight, I'd re-familiarized myself with Squirrel Hill, so I'd be able to map out places to apply for a job.

But before I left the house, I needed to figure out how to get my teacher's certification. As much as I'd like to have some immediate money coming in, I didn't want to spend the next twenty years of my life waiting tables. I needed a career.

Coffee in hand, I opened my laptop, but then peered around the house, surprised at how quiet it was. Raylene wasn't downstairs when I'd made it to the kitchen, so I assumed she'd already left for work. Mom had just finished washing out her mug and was heading to the store.

The only sound that filtered into the house from outside was birdsong, and I was pretty sure that was because my mother had several feeders and birdhouses in the yard.

Only a short jaunt from the city, and yet, my mother owned a little slice of paradise. No wonder she didn't want to leave. I just hoped that I'd be able to find a job soon so I could help her keep this place.

As soon as I logged on, my phone lit up with a text from Joe. He had texted me several times over the weekend, asking when I'd be back, but I'd held off on an answer, wanting to make sure before I jumped. After all, I did still have a place, for at least a month, in New York.

Besides, what was there to talk about anyway? He was moving to Chicago, and someone was moving into his apartment.

Even though I didn't want to respond, I swiped open Joe's message so I could read it. *Alaina, I don't understand why you won't answer me. Did you even read my letter?*

Not wanting to do this, I sighed, but it had to be done. *Are you at home?* I typed.

Yes, I took my vacation over Thanksgiving week so we could talk. Plan.

"Plan? Plan what?" I asked the birds, since they were the only living entities near me, and I didn't want anyone to catch me talking to myself. Talking to myself in New York might not raise heads, but I was sure the people in Pittsburgh might look at me as if I were crazy. I shook the phone as I stared down at his image above the text screen. "You left me. Now you want to plan? Plan what? How to divide the food and toilet paper?" Great! Now I was talking to a phone. I wasn't sure if that was worse than talking to myself or the birds.

It's not as though I had much of anything in his apartment. Maybe that was it. Maybe he needed me to get the rest of my clothes out of the closet.

I hit "call," and waited to see if he'd pick up.

"Thank you!" Joe sounded rushed or frantic, I wasn't sure which, but nothing frazzled Joe, so he must just be in a hurry. "I didn't want to talk with you when you were with your mother, so I was hoping you would call."

"Can't you just put all my stuff in the office, Joe?"

The line was quiet for a second, then a rustling sound came through the line. "What do you mean, Alaina? Aren't you coming home after Thanksgiving? I just assumed you went to see your mom and sister for the holiday. Don't you have to be back for the play?"

A huff escaped my throat. "Home? What do you mean *home*? You left."

"You didn't read my note, did you?" He released a long sigh. "I knew it. I didn't want to believe it, but I knew it."

"Knew what?" I got up from behind my computer and walked to the back porch. "You left, Joe. You didn't even tell me you were considering a job in another state. And I come home to see you leaving. What was I supposed to do?"

"Alaina," Joe said calmly, "do you have the letter?"

I sighed then walked to the table for my bag. I rifled through my oversized satchel that would make Mary Poppins jealous. My bag was large enough that I could have gone years without stumbling over the letter. I practically lived out of my purse, so it was nearly the size of a backpack. "Yes," I finally said when I pulled out the legal-sized envelope with my name written on the outside.

"Would you do me a favor and please call me after you read it?"

My hands broke out in a sweat at his words. Was there something wrong with him, something he couldn't confess in person? "Sure. I guess. What's wrong?"

"Call me right back, okay?"

"Okay, Joe."

The line went silent, and I just stared at the envelope. A few seconds later, I went to sit on my mother's overstuffed chair in the sunroom, the old wingback chair she called her "reading chair." We all knew that when she was in it, she wasn't to be disturbed. Funny how I'd chosen to walk in here and choose her chair, as though I knew the letter would upset me.

I stared down at the innocuous piece of paper as if it might explode. Joe had always been serious, but he'd sounded desperate. And Joe was never anxious about anything. Carefully, I pulled the tab up from its tucked-in position on the back of the envelope, then removed the one page that Joe must have typed out and printed. He'd always complained about his handwriting, even though it was neater than mine by a long shot.

> Dear Alaina,
>
> I know I've been withdrawn the last three months, but that's because I've been waiting to hear news about an amazing opportunity in Chicago. While the position is exactly what I've worked toward for the last ten years, the situation is bittersweet because I know you won't go with me.
>
> I love you, Alaina, but I know your heart and your life belong to the stage. It saddens me because I truly believe that we could be happy forever if you felt the same way about me as I do you.
>
> I'll only be gone for a few days, so I'm asking you to take this time to reflect on our relationship. I know this is the most un-romantic way to do this, and I'm sorry about that, but if I thought there was any chance you would have

said yes, I would have spent any
amount of money to pull off a huge
production and bought you the
grandest diamond imaginable, but I
didn't want to put you on the spot. So,
I'm asking you here, in this stupid
letter. If you love me and want me to
stay in New York, just say the word,
and I will.
Will you marry me?
Yours,
Joe

My heart pounded against my ribcage as I stared down
at the page, shocked. No, flabbergasted. I wasn't sure if
there was a big enough word to describe what I felt.

I dropped my head into my hands. Marry Joe? Stay in
New York? I picked up the phone to hit re-dial, but
inadvertently hit "accept" on an incoming call instead, as
the phone rang in my hands.

Not recognizing the number I'd just hit "accept" on, I
stared down at my phone and considered hanging up.

"Hello? Alaina Ackerman?" a tart female voice called
from the speaker.

I lifted the phone to my ear. "Sorry. Yes, this is Alaina
Ackerman."

"Alaina, this is Michelle with HELL Productions. We
need you to come back to Greensburg. Are you free
today?"

Was this woman kidding? Truly, Fate had a sick sense of
humor, or she just liked to watch me flop around like a fish
out of water. "Ummm … I'm confused." Every other
situation of a callback, I had always answered: *Yes. Of course.
What time?* But I was done. The phone clicked with an
incoming call. I peeked at the phone to see Joe's name. I

wrestled with asking the woman to hold while I accepted his call, but curiosity got the best of me. I could call Joe back in a few minutes. "I thought all the parts had been filled."

"Well, yes. They were." A clicking sound filtered through the phone as though she were tapping her desk with a pen. *The blonde in the thousand-dollar pantsuit*, I realized. "Until this morning, that is. The lead role has just opened up. The woman we chose failed her background check, and Howard is a stickler about having any marks on your portfolio. Tell me, Ms. Ackerman, have you ever been filmed in the nude or been arrested?"

"Of course not," I exclaimed, offended.

"Not even by an ex-boyfriend? It's amazing how dicey images suddenly show up the moment a *nobody* is offered a lead role."

I couldn't believe I was listening to this, especially since I wasn't accepting a role anyway. But I still wanted to prove to this woman that they'd chosen the wrong woman. "No. Never."

"Good. When can you come to Greensburg?"

I spurted out a laugh. This woman was a piece of work. No wonder she could afford a thousand-dollar pantsuit. "With all due respect, Michelle, I've been to Greensburg three times. The CD said he had my audition taped and didn't need to see me audition again —"

"Understood, Alaina," she cut me off, "but you won't be auditioning for the CD; you will be personally auditioning for Howard Edwards the Second."

My eyes instantly watered up, which told me two things. One, I had to go, and two, Joe was right. I loved Joe, but Joe asking me to marry him hadn't brought tears to my eyes. Then again, if he'd said the same words to me in person — or before I'd left New York — maybe they would have. Or even on the phone. But no, he'd not wanted to waste money on anything extravagant if I might have said no.

Markus's face — along with Buddy's sad puppy eyes — popped into my head, though. I couldn't shake the image of how utterly honest Markus had looked when he'd said he'd give me forever if I stayed in Pittsburgh. Would my landing a lead role in a major motion picture make him happy or sad? Other actresses managed a personal life and a career, though. Why did it feel like I had to make a choice between one or the other?

"What time would you like me there?"

Chapter 12 – That Old Harpy Fate

Before I moved from my chair, I sent Joe a text. *I can't talk right now. I really have to think about your letter. I'll call you back later.*

It wasn't that I wanted to lead Joe on. I did love him, and I did have to think about his … proposal, although it certainly didn't feel like a proposal. The fact of the matter is … I had loved my life in New York, but did that mean I loved Joe? My feelings were confusing, to say the least. I knew without a doubt that I cared about Joe, but was that enough? Joe's kiss and touch didn't make my toes curl like when Markus touched me. If that was all I had with Markus, I knew for certain it wouldn't be enough, but we had more. We had history, and we were still good friends.

My head was too cluttered to think about Joe and Markus right now. I had one last audition to make, and since I'd called AAA and had them install a new battery in the Taurus, I didn't have to call my mother or Markus for a ride. Nor did I have to tell either of them that I was heading to Greensburg for a fourth time.

If Howard didn't show, or I didn't get the role, no one had to know I'd even gone. I felt like a whipped dog crawling back to her master with her tail between her legs. Only, I really was done. I absolutely refused to take any crap this time.

For the first time in my long career, I felt liberated, felt as though I were free to say, *Take this part and shove it!* Definitely couldn't hurt at this point. Being polite hadn't earned me any roles. Maybe I needed to start being more difficult ... more like Michelle appeared to be.

Once again, I sat in a barren, windowless room with twelve other women, all in their early to late thirties, and all rehearsing the same lines I would hopefully get to speak today. Other than plastic chairs and a desk at the front, the room didn't even have pictures.

To pass the time, I counted the ceiling tiles a hundred or so times, and when I still hadn't been called, I switched to counting the divots within each tile as I thought about my lines and how they correlated with my life. How my chosen career path had squeezed every bit of life out of me until there was nothing left.

I didn't have my *sides*, since I had thrown them away after the last letdown, but I didn't need them. I'd sat here so many hours studying them that I was positive I wouldn't forget them for the rest of my life, just like my high school play. Certain lines just stuck with me, like a jingle I couldn't shake.

One by one, the monitor led women to the next room. Once again, I was one of the last women in the room. Did that mean Howard would leave before I had a chance to read my lines again? Everything in me told me I should just leave now, but I decided not to. Instead, I rehearsed what I'd say if I heard, "We'll let you know …"

The words that entered my mind actually made me smile, boosting my confidence. I'd never spoken back to anyone, ever. Not even to rude customers. I'd always just accepted whatever the casting directors, customers, and employers had to say.

But not today. Today, I would go out with a bang, so I'd have something to talk about for the rest of my life. I would make sure to take a mental image of the shocked faces. Maybe they'll be recording the auditions today, and my *momentary lapse of reason* will end up on YouTube as a disgruntled actress, like the outtakes from *American Idol*.

Just thinking about it made me giggle beneath my breath, causing the last few women in front of me to turn around in their chairs.

"Sorry …" I said. "Just remembered something funny."

Without a word, each of them went back to rehearsing their lines.

Everything in me wanted to break out in more giggles … or maybe in a song, since *Take this Job and Shove It* had been playing in my head since I'd thought about it earlier. Only, I continued to replace the word *Job* with *Part*. It'd be a perfect chance to show Howard that I could hold a tune, too.

An hour later, I was the only one left in the room. Even the monitor had been gone for several minutes.

Finally, the door opened, and the monitor summoned me with the crook of her finger.

I followed, finding myself on the massive stage again, the lights brighter than the first three times I'd stood in the same spot.

The reader walked center stage, his face bored, just like every reader I'd ever worked with. I was pretty sure it was their job to speak as monotone as possible, to see if the actor would be able to work when given nothing but words.

The CD gave his cue, and the reader turned to me, "Why are you here?"

To land this role, or to tell off your crew, I thought angrily, but stuck to my line. "To get stronger," I droned. When the character had responded in the book, she was timid, meek, depressed, tired. The way I felt right now. Her tone hadn't been mad.

"Why?" The reader's voice was flat.

"Because I don't want to be weak," I said, still soft, but I stood taller. I wasn't weak. I refused to be weak. I'd wasted twenty years being weak.

"Why?" he demanded.

"Because I don't want to be afraid," I said louder. I wasn't afraid of these haughty people anymore. *I don't need this part. I have a home, a family, and a man who loves me — actually two men claimed to love me. And Buddy.*

"Afraid of what?"

You! I wanted to scream, but I growled, "Everything!" *Everything about this business that squeezed the life out of me for the last twenty years, I wanted to say*, but I was pretty sure I didn't need to say it. Based on the reader's eyes, my expression said everything that I didn't.

"Then let me see you."

I shifted my stance as I'd learned in the kickboxing classes I'd taken over the years. I imagined Howard Edwards's face and thrusted my fist forward with a *rebel yell* as though I'd made contact with his nose and shoved the bone through his brain.

"Again. Harder."

I struck air again, harder this time, then released my best kick-to-the-groin move to the invisible entity in front of me.

"Face your fear," the reader said, and I instantly visualized my mother telling me not to give up on my dream. But no matter what happened, I'd never be a slave to my career again.

"I hate you! I hate you!" I screamed, pummeling the faces of twenty years of casting directors. I would do this. I would take control of the rest of my life and not let any CD, director, or producer ever make me feel as though I weren't good enough ever again.

The reader got up in my face. "Give your fear a name."

"Loneliness!" I wailed. "I don't want to be afraid to be alone!" And I didn't. I didn't want to put my career in front of my happiness ever again. *If I landed the part, fine, but my health and my family would come first,* I silently avowed.

The reader actually flashed me a small smile, then looked to the CD.

Exhausted from the small amount of exercise, especially after I'd gorged myself all weekend, I inhaled quietly, attempting to catch my breath in case I had to say something else.

A man stepped to the side of the bright spotlight. *Clap, clap, clap.* I blinked, attempting to see beyond the white starbursts blinding me. The man was tall, had salt-and-pepper hair. Howard. I'd forgotten to look for him this time. I was just happy I was finally allowed to say my lines on stage, and worrying about whether Howard was watching hadn't crossed my mind.

Wait! What just happened? Was Howard clapping for me?

Howard stepped forward a few feet again, then cocked his head ever so slightly, the way he'd done on the outside patio last week. He looked down at his clipboard, then back up at me. "Ackerman? Do you live in Squirrel Hill?"

Shocked, I stepped forward. Was I supposed to bow? I mean ... he was known as one of the best producers in the world, and he was talking to me, *a nobody*, as Michelle had so eloquently put it. "Ummm ..." Damn. Why had I stuttered? "Yes, sir. Well, technically, I live in New York, but I was born in Squirrel Hill. My mother still lives there." And now I was blathering like an idiot.

One side of Howard's face lifted, and he gave me a soft nod. "I thought I recognized the name."

"Oh, yes. A friend of mine said you grew up in Squirrel Hill."

Howard raised his eyebrows. "A friend?"

"Yeah. Ummm ..." Damn. Stuttering again. "Klein. Markus Klein. His father knew your father, said he helped find you a house." *Connections, no matter how small,* my last agent had told me. *Anything that makes them remember you.*

Howard nodded. "Yes, he did." Howard looked as though he wanted to say something else, but then he shook it off. Literally. He walked to the CD, spoke a few words that I couldn't hear, and then looked back up at me. "Great job, Ms. Ackerman. As long as your background check goes through, the role is yours."

What? Just like that? No waiting by the phone for weeks on end? I cleared my throat. "Thank you."

"Enjoy the Thanksgiving holiday. We'll be in contact next week," the CD added, dismissing me.

I blew out a breath as I attempted to hold back my tears. My cheeks lifted, seemingly of their own accord, which seemed to make it even harder not to cry. I whirled, looking for the exit, and the reader caught my eye, and smiled. He pointed to something behind me.

I turned and saw the door, then turned back to him. "Thank you," I whispered.

He simply nodded. I had a sneaking suspicion he was part of the reason I got another chance.

I scooped up my purse and ran through the corridor to the exit, anxious to get outside, so I could cry, scream, howl, dance … all of the above.

At the glass doors by the old-fashioned ticket booth, I whirled around to see the posters for upcoming plays and events, and couldn't stop the tears as I glanced at each one. My name would be on a movie poster.

"I did it, Zayde. Mom. I did it!" I bit down on my lip to hold back any more outbursts.

Since the tears refused to stop, I hurried out of the theater and rushed down the sidewalk for the car. I tugged the door open and fell into the seat, not even caring if the Taurus refused to start, since I wouldn't be able to drive for a few minutes in my condition anyway.

"The lead in a major motion picture!" I screamed, looking at the roof of the Taurus. "Thank you! Thank you! Thank you!"

As every other man, woman, and child in the world can attest, including Jane Austen and Bridget Jones, it is a truth universally acknowledged that the moment something great happens in your life, something awful is sure to follow.

That's the only thing I could think of when I walked into the house and heard someone puking.

I had known something was wrong. I'd tried to ignore it, but deep down, I'd seen the signs:

Mom reminding me that I hadn't been home for a holiday in years. Mom shaking her head for me to drop my questions about Russell. The insistence that I was needed, when I'd never been needed by either of them. My entire life, I'd been the needy one.

As quietly as I could, I ascended the stairs.

She was there, hunched over the toilet.

I leapt forward and pulled her chestnut hair away from the toilet, the way she'd done for me on nights when I'd been too young and had drunk too much, and ended up hugging the toilet all night.

When she finished, I reached for a towel, then supported her body, which felt so light, even though she'd always been larger than me, and escorted her back to her bed.

"I'm sorry," my sister had the nerve to say.

"What is it, Ray? Why haven't you told me that you were sick?"

She reached up and brushed away the tears that were falling down my cheeks. "I didn't want you to worry. Didn't want you to feel you had to come back for me."

"What's wrong?"

"It's not the sickness as much as it is the treatment. I have stage III breast cancer. My doctor has been trying to shrink the tumors enough that I can have a breast-conserving surgery, but it's no use —" Her voice cracked on a cry. "I'm going to lose both of my breasts, Lain. He says he has to perform a double mastectomy on me, said it's my only chance."

"Oh, Raylene!" I hugged her against my body. "I'm so sorry."

Her frail body shook as I held her.

"I'll take care of you, Ray. I promise. I'll move back home permanently and take care of you."

Chapter 13 – Rejecting the Dream

Michelle's voicemail picked up, stating that she wouldn't be returning calls until next week. Of course, the Thanksgiving holiday.

The line beeped, and I froze. I didn't even know Michelle's last name.

"Ummm …" I rolled my eyes at my stuttering again. "Michelle, this is Alaina Ackerman. I know the CD said he would call me after you ran a background check, but I didn't want you to waste the money, since I can't accept the role. I have an emergency in the family, so I will have to pass on this opportunity. Please thank Howard Edwards for offering me the chance at a lead role, but I simply cannot accept right now. Thank you. Bye."

I clicked *End* on the phone and then just let my arms fall to my sides as I inhaled and exhaled a long breath. "That's it then. The deed is done."

"Call her back!" Raylene demanded from behind me.

Ignoring my sister, I lifted my phone and clicked the *Command* button, then touched the *Phone* tab. I swiped away the sent call and the received call from Michelle, making the phone number disappear immediately. "I can't," I said as I turned to Raylene. "I just deleted the phone number."

Raylene grabbed the phone out of my hands and glared at the screen. "What is wrong with you?"

I bit down on my lip and shook my head. "*Nothing's* wrong with me."

"That's not funny, Alaina." Raylene staggered backward, so I reached out and steadied her, then led her to the sofa. "I'm fine!" she barked. "I don't want you to do this; I don't want you to sacrifice your dream because of me. This …" She fluttered her hands in front of her body. "This'll pass."

I sat down beside my sister, and she wrapped her arms around me, the way she had when Daddy had died, then Bubbie, then Zayde. Raylene had always been there for me when our mother had to work. The least I could do was help her when she needed me for the first time in our lives.

Other than our sniffles and the soft tick of the clock on the mantel, the house was utterly quiet. Eerily quiet. I'd missed this solitude, though. In New York, my mind felt as though it worked 24/7, since even when I slept, I could hear the sounds of the city.

Raylene released a long, exhausted breath and I pulled back to look at her. "I got what I wanted, Ray. I landed the lead part in a major motion picture. I never said I had to actually perform the role."

She choked out a half-laugh, half-cry. "Thank you, Laina, but it'll be fine. I'll have the surgery, and then I'll be fine."

"Liar …" I said. "I spent the last hour researching stage III cancer. I'm sure you know more than I do, but from everything I read, you'll need more chemo after the surgery, too. Which means you'll continue to be sick. And look at you … you're skin and bones now."

"Gee thanks." Raylene raised her arm to smack me, but then dropped her hand back in her lap as though she didn't even have the strength to hold up her arm.

I pulled back and stared her in the eyes, the way she'd done to me so many times when she was taking control of a situation. "First things first, I'm moving you into Zayde's room. You have no business walking up three flights of stairs. I'll have all of your stuff moved down tonight. Then, I'm going to make you a pot of chicken and rice soup. You're not working, I take it?"

Raylene shook her head. "I had to take a medical leave of absence. I'm just too weak."

"It's okay. I'll get a job waiting tables at night so I can be here during the day, then Mom can be here with you at night."

My sister smiled, but it was a feeble effort, worse than her attempt at smacking me. "Alaina, please don't give up because of me."

"I was giving up anyway," I said. "I only went to that stupid audition because Mom asked me to go. And hey, I get to go out knowing I turned down Howard Edwards the Second. How many women can say that?"

Raylene actually burst out a laugh this time. "Not too many. Only an Ackerman woman would do that."

"Damn straight!" I said. "Okay. You lie down here. I'm going to make you something to eat, then start on your room." I forced a smile and then hopped up and headed to the kitchen.

"Alaina ..."

I turned. "Yes?"

"Thank you."

"What are sisters for?"

She nodded, pulled the afghan off the back of the sofa, and then rested her head on one of the round pillows Bubbie had made.

It took every ounce of power I had, but I absolutely refused to cry. I would be strong for Raylene.

The door swung open just as I'd squatted down in front of the kitchen cabinet. Buddy came running across the floor, all wiggles and wags, making a beeline straight for me.

My hands automatically wrapped around him, and I stood, clutching him to my chest. Buddy kept still, simply lifting his head so he could lick the bottom of my chin, as if he knew I was upset. Then Markus wrapped his arms around me, and the tears fell. I held back the audible cries, though. I might not be able to stop the stupid waterworks, but I refused to let Raylene hear me. I wanted her to be able to count on me.

Markus ran his fingers across my cheeks. "I'm sorry."

"How did you know?" I whispered. When we'd talked yesterday, Markus had said that he couldn't make it until after five tonight.

"Ray texted me."

"Why didn't you tell me?" I was angry that my mother and sister had told Markus but not me, but I didn't have room in my heart for anger. No, my heart was filled to the brim with anguish for my sister.

"She made me promise," Markus said, kissing my forehead. "I'm sorry. I know it was wrong, but I also had to respect Ray's feelings. We've become good friends over the years."

"I noticed." I sniffed. "Nothing else, though?" The last thing I wanted to do was take that from my sister, too. If she was in love with Markus, I'd step back.

"No … never. I only have eyes for you. I've never stopped loving you, Laina."

I set Buddy on the floor and threw my arms around Markus. "I'm sorry."

"No need to be sorry. It's my fault. I let you go. I never told you." Markus touched me under the chin. "But I'm telling you now. I love you, Alaina. I don't want you to leave, but if you decide to go back to New York, or Hollywood, or Timbuktu for that matter, I'll go with you if you'll have me."

"Really?"

"Really. If you feel the same way about me. If you love me and want me with you, that is. I'm a writer. I can write anywhere in the world."

"I'm not going anywhere, Markus. I'm staying right here in Squirrel Hill so I can take care of my sister."

He smiled softly. "And after that …?"

"I guess we'll just have to see what happens after that."

"Works for me." Markus pressed his lips against mine, but then Buddy wriggled his way between our legs. "I better take him outside."

I sniffed again, trying to catch my breath. "I need to make something for Ray to eat anyway. Are you hungry?"

"Always." He winked. "What did you have in mind?"

"Chicken soup."

"Oh, well … that works too, I guess."

"Go take him outside. I have work for you when you get back."

"Yes, Ma'am!"

After Markus and I had moved most of my sister's things to the only bedroom on the first floor, I woke Raylene for dinner.

Raylene, as pale and thin as she was, didn't look weak as she sat across from me at the dinner table. She rapidly tapped just her thumb against the glossy cherry-stained tabletop, as if contemplating her next move. "Did she tell you the news?"

"Did who tell us what news?" my mother asked.

My sister picked up her spoon and pointed it at me. "Her. Your prodigal daughter."

Markus looked at me, then at Raylene, his brow furrowing at once. "Tell us what?"

Raylene started to answer, but I cut her off. "Calling me names isn't going to change my mind, Sis. I'm staying and that's the end of it."

Markus chuckled, then looked between Raylene and me for clarification. "Not my place, of course, but isn't that a good thing? Laina wanting to stay?"

"Not if she has to sacrifice her dreams for it," Raylene growled.

"Ray," I sighed, "I told you. I'm happy. This is what I want."

My mother set down her fork and stared at me now. "What is Ray talking about, Laina?"

"Laina landed the lead in *You Don't Need a Man*, but called back and turned it down after she discovered I was sick."

My mother furrowed her brow as she stared at me. "Is that true, Alaina?"

I exhaled a huge gust of air. "Yes. Yes. I don't understand you people. First, everyone is upset because I don't live here, and now everyone's upset because I said I want to stay." I slid my chair back and jumped up from the table, then darted for the stairs, the way I'd done when I was a teenager. Halfway up the stairs, I realized Buddy was on my heels, doing his best to climb the steps. I reached down and scooped him up, then charged up to my room.

"What do they want from me, boy? Why are they never happy?"

His tail thumped against my arm, but he had no answer.

"What do you think I should do?"

Buddy nuzzled his head closer to my chin, so I squeezed him, then set him down. It had always amazed me that animals looked humans in the eyes. How did they know that?

I sat down beside him, and he hopped onto my lap.

"You are a good boy, aren't you? Why isn't someone looking for you?" Was there something wrong with him? I had to agree with my mother: Why would someone let a perfectly good *anything* go?

A soft tap on the door caused Buddy to jump out of my lap and yip. "Ahh … and you're a watch dog, too. Perfect."

The handle turned, but Buddy stood his ground. When the door inched open, Buddy remained vigilant, but backed up a few inches.

"Laina?" Markus asked as he tapped on the door while opening it at the same time.

Buddy ran to greet him.

"Traitor," I mumbled. "We're mad at all of them, remember?"

At the sound of my voice, Buddy ran back to me, but then stopped between the two of us.

"He's torn," Markus said.

"I know the feeling."

Markus walked to where I sat on the floor and lowered himself beside me, which pleased Buddy. He immediately curled up between us. "I think he thinks we both belong to him."

I looked up at Markus and shook my head. "You're ruthless."

"No, really. Every time we're together, he rests silently between us, but when you run off, he jumps up. His comfortable world ends the moment you're sad."

I sighed, realizing I'd done that to Markus repeatedly. Every time he started to get comfortable, I'd jump up and leave him.

"I'm not going anywhere, Markus. I already turned down the role. I'm staying here."

Markus released a long breath. "But you'll be unhappy."

"I won't be unhappy. I'm turning forty in a few months. I'm tired of running around. I want to settle down."

Markus leaned forward, and I closed the distance. He wrapped his hand around the back of my neck and coaxed me closer. I opened up to him. His warmth. His smell. His kiss. Markus really did feel like home.

I hated that I'd had to make a choice, but I'd made up my mind. I simply wasn't willing to leave my mother and sister alone, and I was in love with Markus.

I leaned back and looked at the man I'd been in love with my entire life. "I love you, Markus, and I'm staying. We'll figure out everything else as we go along."

"I love you, too, Alaina, but you already knew that. And as I said earlier, stay or leave, we *will* figure out everything else, because I'm never letting you go again without a fight."

Chapter 14 – Sisters

As always, other than the birdsong and the ticking of the clock, the house was utterly quiet when I came downstairs.

But unlike the previous days, there was a major difference in the kitchen. My sister. Wrapped up in an old patchwork quilt that Bubbie had made years ago, Raylene sat with her back to me, just staring out the glass door into the backyard. Now that I knew she wasn't working, I guessed she didn't have to hide from me.

"It's so peaceful, isn't it?" Raylene said without moving from her cocooned state. "I never took the time to do this. Never took the time just to sip tea and listen to the birds. Every day was packed from the time I woke up, until I fell into bed at night."

I leaned over the back of the chair and draped my arms around her, resting my chin on her shoulder.

Raylene leaned into me. "You know, everyone always said I had my life figured out, that I was so smart, so successful. But what is success, anyway? Working your way up to a branch manager position, starring in a movie, or choosing to have a child and stay home? How can anyone really measure what success is?"

I straightened my back and walked around my sister, pulling a chair from the table to sit beside her. "I don't know. I always thought you were successful."

She turned to me. "And I envied you."

"What? Why?"

"For being brave. For not being afraid to live month to month."

I laughed. "Gee. Thanks."

Raylene struggled to sit up in her chair without breaking her cocoon. "No, really. I know there's something to be said for both lives, but think of all the places you've been because you weren't tied down to a job."

True. Whenever a friend of mine was starring somewhere, I could grab a cheap flight and go visit them since I had a free place to stay. Other than New York, I'd spent time in L.A., San Francisco, Phoenix, Florida, North Carolina, Chicago … even Japan. Raylene knew that, of course. I'd never thought it was bragging when I posted images to my Facebook page.

"But you were happy, right?" I asked. "With Russell. What happened?"

She dropped her head. "Yes … Until …" She sniffed, and I was sorry I'd asked. I'd kept my mouth shut ever since Mom had suggested I not talk about it. I'd been waiting for Raylene to open up to me. "The moment he found out I had breast cancer, he said it was over, said he wasn't ready for that. Especially since there was a good chance I'd lose my breasts."

I gasped. "He didn't! What a —" I suppressed my expletive at the hurt look in Raylene's eyes.

"He did. Days later, he refinanced the house so he could buy me out of my half because he was afraid that debtors would come after the property when my insurance ran out."

"Has it run out?" I asked, concerned at once. What would happen if she couldn't get the treatment she needed?

"No. One of the benefits of working eighty hours a week for so many years. But, it all depends on how much chemo I need after the surgery."

"Oh, Ray," I said. "I'm so sorry. I wish there was something I could say or do."

She shrugged. "There isn't. This is life. I'm not the first woman to deal with this. Thankfully, I do have great health coverage, and Mom, of course. I don't know what I would have done without her." Raylene stared up at me. "I'm sorry she called you home, Laina. She was scared. Scared that something would happen to me during the operation, and then you'd be upset at her for not telling you that I was sick."

I narrowed my eyes. "I would have been. I am mad. You had no right to keep that from me. I'm your sister, and like you said, my job enables me to be here. You just had to let me know," I said, exasperated. I sniffed, attempting to hold back the tears. "When's the surgery?"

"Not until after the holidays. Isn't that nice? I get to keep my womanhood for one more Christmas. Of course, I'm losing more of my hair every day and sicker than a dog from the chemo, which doesn't seem to be working anyway."

I blew out a long breath. I wanted to say that her breasts weren't what made her a woman, but I tried to imagine myself in her position, and how stupid I would think the woman was who would dare say that to a woman who was losing her breasts. Her breasts *weren't* what made her a woman, of course, but it would still sound thoughtless coming from a woman who had her breasts, so the only thing I said was the truth, "I'm so sorry, Ray ..."

Now Raylene sniffed. "And I'm afraid."

I jumped out of my chair and lowered my body over hers. "I'll be here. The way you've always been here for me. You can count on me."

Raylene buried her head into my shoulder. "Thank you. I really don't want you to miss your chance at your dream, but thank you for coming home, Laina."

I leaned back. "It was time for me to come home. Besides, if I hadn't come home, I wouldn't have landed a lead role."

"A role you're not taking because of me."

"Not just you. Mom, Markus, Buddy ... I have lots of reasons to stay home."

"And what about Joe? I never thought he was your type, but when I saw you together in New York, he seemed crazy about you."

My sister was nothing if not perceptive. Maybe because she didn't ramble on as I did. Instead, she'd be the one to sit back and analyze a situation, people. In the end, she probably walked away from a conversation knowing more about a person than the person knew about him- or herself.

"Joe ... Hmmm ... He asked me to marry him. Can you believe it?"

"And what did you say?"

I flopped back down in my chair again. "He asked me in a letter, a letter he left on the counter because he was accepting a job in Chicago. Apparently, he didn't think I loved him, so he didn't want to go through the fanfare and money of asking me in an extravagant way. He said if I agreed to marry him he'd stay in New York, though."

"When did this happen?"

I couldn't stop the bitter chuckle that escaped my mouth. "He left the letter for me the day I came here … but I didn't read it until right before I got the final callback for the audition. Like I said, I had several reasons to come home, but I have more reasons to stay."

Raylene's eyes were thoughtful. "But do you love Joe?"

At Raylene's penetrating gaze, I thought long and hard about my answer. Clearly, she was hurt by Russell's rejection. "Yes, I do love Joe, but I don't think I love him enough to marry him. I think …" I paused as I thought through my words again. "I know it's only been a little over a week. Well, thirty-three years plus a little over a week, but I think I'm in love with Markus. Like, really in love, not just, 'he's a friend I care about' kind of love, but an 'I think I want to spend the rest of my life with him' kind of love."

Raylene smiled. I loved seeing my sister smile, something she didn't do often enough, even when she wasn't sick. "Markus loves you, Laina. He really, really loves you. You should see the way he smiles whenever he talks about you. His entire face lights up. And when Mom told him you might be coming home for Thanksgiving after she spoke with you, she said she thought he might have even teared up."

I sighed. "It's scary, though. I mean, just a little over a week ago, I was in a relationship for three years, and I walked away without even a tear. I mean, I was sad. I was ticked, but I didn't cry. What does that say about me?"

My sister's lips turned up slightly. "I don't want to tell you what you feel, as only you know that, but, I think it means you cared for Joe, but I don't think you *really* loved him."

"That makes me sound so, so … I don't even want to think about what that makes me feel like. I certainly don't want to make that same mistake again. And definitely not with Markus."

"Markus won't push you. He never has before."

"No, Markus has never pushed me for anything."

But maybe he should have ...

Chapter 15 – Station Square

The phone rang and I just stared at it, trying to make out the name of the caller through hazy eyes.

Raylene and I had talked through the day and into the night, catching up on years and years of missed events. While we'd spent many holidays together, and had talked on the phone nearly monthly, there was nothing like sitting face to face, confessing and sharing dreams and secrets, regrets and hope.

Through one eye, I read Markus's name and clicked *Answer*. "I'm only answering this because it's you, you know."

"Thank you. I'm glad I rate high enough on your *Friends* list to rate an answer."

I groaned at his chipper tone so early in the morning.

"Good morning to you too, sunshine. It's my day off, and Buddy and I would like to spend it with you."

"Doing what?" I mumbled.

"Oh, we have to qualify there too?"

I laughed. "No, I'm just tired. Ray and I stayed up all night talking."

"Hmm … I was thinking since it was Thanksgiving tomorrow, and you were complaining how much you'd eaten in the last few days, I thought we'd go to another park, several actually. I have the entire day mapped out for dog-friendly activities."

"What's the weather like?"

"Just checked. Sunny and sixty. Perfect. But bring a jacket."

"Okay, give me an hour to get ready."

"You got it. I can knock out a few more words, then."

"I thought today was your day off."

"It is. This isn't work. This is something else I've been working on."

"Oh. All right. See you in an hour." And I hung up.

Before moving out of bed, though, I just sat with my head between my knees, thinking about my sister. Would she be okay by herself?

Instead of heading to the shower, I headed downstairs to her room. "Ray," I tapped on the door.

"Come in."

Ray was sitting by the window, sipping tea. She looked good, better than she had since I'd been here. "You look good today."

"It comes and goes. They have me on a cycle of treatments. I don't start up again until next week, so hopefully I can enjoy Thanksgiving tomorrow." She lifted the cup to her mouth and sipped. "The ginger tea helps too. Amazing stuff, really."

"I've heard that it helps stress, too, or maybe that's just because many people confuse an upset stomach with anxiety." I sat down on the window ledge. "Markus wants me to go out with him today, but —"

"I'm fine, Laina. Great, really. Go. Have fun. I'll call you if I start to feel ill."

"You sure?"

"Yes, I'm sure. I'm just going to read."

I walked over to her and kissed her forehead. "Okay. Please call me if you need me. We won't be far, I'm sure. And I'll make sure I take you to all of your appointments from now on, so you won't have to go alone. I promise."

"I haven't been alone. Mom's been taking me, the reason Markus has been filling in so much. But that'll be great. It's hard on her. You know how much she hates to drive to Pittsburgh."

I laughed. "Yeah, especially when the tunnel monsters are causing traffic to back up."

"Exactly," Raylene said through a reserved chuckle.

Markus paid to park in a parking garage downtown, then we walked down a level from the street to the subway, Buddy tucked quietly in a carrier.

"You won't be able to carry him like that for long, will you?" I said.

Markus smiled. "No, *we* won't."

Had I heard right? Had Markus emphasized the word, *we*?

"That's why I wanted to do this now, before he gets too big."

"So, you're keeping him?"

Markus looked at me and grinned. "No, I'm training him. You're keeping him. In fact, he's almost completely trained, so I think tomorrow he'll move in with you. He needs more room to run."

I stared at Buddy's sad eyes as I sat down on a bench seat on the train ... He definitely had the expressive round eyes of a boxer. "You want to move in with me, Buddy?" His tail smacked against the crate.

Markus stuck his hand inside the crate and stroked Buddy on the neck. "Of course he does; he loves you. He wants to be with you all the time."

"And what about you?"

Markus sat down beside me. "Do I want to move in with you?"

"No," I said through a nervous chuckle. "I meant, won't he miss you, since you've spent more time with him than I have?"

"Well, I was kind of hoping I'd have visitation rights. You know, since I'm a great father and all." Markus leaned toward me and kissed my cheek. "And since I am in love with his mommy."

I peeked up at Markus from beneath my lashes, but then my built-in Markus-meter went off, offering me a chance to protect myself from getting lost in the romantic moment. "As if any of that mattered; you've been able to come and go in my house since we were seven years old."

"That's true."

The overhead recorder announced Point Park, and Markus readied us to leave the train.

The park, located at the confluence of three rivers in downtown Pittsburgh, not only had a historic blockhouse from the French and Indian War, but also boasted beautiful landscaping and a 100-foot water fountain.

Markus hooked the leash to Buddy's collar, then set him on the grass. Buddy took one look at the wide open stretch of grass and bolted, only to reach the end of his leash in seconds. "What did I tell you about that? You promised to show Laina how well trained you are." Buddy sat, and Markus rolled out a towel on the grass. "You lie back while I go wear him out."

"Sounds like a deal." I lowered myself to the towel and watched as Markus ran with Buddy, careful to hold the leash away from his legs.

I raised my head to the sun. It was cool, but the clear, sunny day made it feel perfect. Pittsburgh really did have amazing weather. Yeah, it got cold, but even that was beautiful.

My phone chimed, and I pulled it out immediately, hoping Raylene was okay.

Not Raylene. Joe. I stared at the text. *Are you coming home for Thanksgiving or staying with your family in Pittsburgh? I really want to talk to you, Alaina.*

Home? Why had Joe seemed to forget that he left home? Left me?

I'm sorry I haven't called. I've just been so busy. I'll call you on Friday.

Okay. Happy Thanksgiving. I love you. Tell your mother and Ray I said hi.

I shoved the phone back in my purse. I'd meant to call him, but there never seemed to be a good time since Raylene wasn't hiding anymore. Why was Joe doing this all of a sudden? For three months I'd thought our relationship was over. Yeah, we'd lived together, but he'd pulled so far away I'd thought he was indifferent. Now, I had to hear that he'd thought I was indifferent.

I sighed, wondering if I would have felt differently about his proposal if he'd delivered it in person.

"Whew!" Markus whooshed out a breath. "If you ever want to burn calories, try keeping up with Buddy."

I laughed. "I noticed." I moved over so Markus could sit beside me.

He sat down, immediately wrapping his arm around me. Then, as before, Buddy settled down between us. Markus reached down and ruffled him between the ears. "Happy?"

I knew Markus was talking to Buddy, but I leaned my head on Markus's shoulder. "I am." And I was suddenly grateful Joe hadn't asked me to marry him in New York. Coming home was the best decision I'd ever made. I'd have to sneak away and call Joe right after Thanksgiving. It wouldn't be right to officially break up with him on a holiday.

Markus rested his head against mine. "Me too."

From Point Park, we rode the train to Station Square.

Another fountain was the main event of the riverfront attraction, only the fountain at Station Square danced to the music.

Buddy enjoyed running back and forth with the dozen or so kids, which meant Markus had to run with him, and I couldn't help but think again what a great father Markus would be. I suddenly wondered if I would have been a good mother, something I'd never thought about.

I'd thought about having kids, of course; I'd just never thought about what kind of mother I would have been.

Markus ran up to me, as did Buddy, who decided to shake the water off his fur at that exact moment.

"Yikes! That's freezing."

Markus took advantage of my freezing comment and sat down beside me, wrapping both his arms around me. "Better?"

"Always. You're like my own personal space heater."

"And I don't even steal the covers …"

I narrowed my eyes, thinking back to a few nights ago when I'd stayed at his place all night. He *hadn't* stolen the covers. Raylene said Markus wouldn't push me, but he did.

He constantly pushed me with subtle innuendoes, making me burn inside. But ... I couldn't take our relationship to the next level until I officially broke off my relationship with Joe. While, I thought it'd been clear that we were over the moment Joe took off for Chicago, his letter said otherwise.

Ignoring my gaze, Markus smiled. "Hungry?"

"Yes." I laughed. I was definitely hungry.

"What did I say?"

I dropped my head. "Nothing. You didn't say anything ... I was just ... Never mind. Let's eat."

I wanted to say, *I know I'm falling in love with you ...*

But I couldn't say that. Because as soon as I said it, that stupid director of fate would yell, *Cut. Cut. Cut. We can't have her falling in love this early on. That's not exciting enough. How 'bout we have the train derail in front of the restaurant ...*

Chapter 16 – Fate Doesn't Take a Holiday

Not sure why, but for some crazy reason, I told my mother and sister that I would take care of everything for Thanksgiving dinner, which meant I'd gotten up before the crack of dawn to get the pumpkin pie cooked and out of the oven before I had to put the turkey in the oven. Then I'd spent hours prepping the potatoes, stuffing, cranberry sauce and, of course, all the snacks that we'd munch on throughout the day.

Then it was time to get cleaned up and take a nap before Markus came over. If this was going to be anything like our Thanksgiving holidays throughout the years, we'd be up all night playing cards and then hit the stores at seven a.m. for all the Black Friday deals. That had been the tradition as long as I could remember.

Showered and changed, I headed downstairs to turn on the TV and take a nap on the couch. Nothing said *nap* like the sound of football in the background.

The doorbell rang, so I headed toward the front door. It was only eleven, and I'd told Markus to come over at noon — I stopped in my tracks. Wait. Markus never came to the front door. Now hesitant, I made my way quietly to the front door. I couldn't imagine that a salesman would come on Thanksgiving, but I didn't want him to see me, or I'd feel compelled to answer the door.

A peek through the peephole revealed the back of a man dressed in a dark suit. He didn't seem to be holding a vacuum cleaner or literature. "Hello?" I called through the door. I never answered the door for strangers, no matter how nicely dressed.

The man turned at the sound of my voice. "Alaina?"

"Joe?" I unlocked the deadbolt and opened the door. "What are you doing here?"

He huffed out a laugh. "Nice to see you too. It's Thanksgiving. And since you haven't found time to talk to me, I figured I'd drive to you for my answer."

"You drove?"

"Yes. Can I come in?"

I wagged my head. "Oh, yes. Sorry." I stepped back inside so he could come in.

Joe wiped his feet and stepped inside, then took me into his arms, planting a kiss on my lips so quickly I had no time to respond.

"Oh …" I said stepping back. "Wow. I can't believe you drove all this way to talk."

Joe forced a smile, but it was weak. "Not just to talk. I screwed up. I know that now." He reached into his pocket and pulled out a black box.

"Oh, Joe … Ummm …" I stuttered.

Joe dropped to his knees on my mother's Oriental rug. "I love you, Alaina, and I'm sorry if I didn't make that clear to you. I just didn't want to make a mistake like I did last time. But the time apart from you … It's been hell. Please say you'll be my wife. We'll stay in New York, if it makes you happy. Anything, just say the word." Joe flicked open the velvet box, revealing a dazzling diamond ring that had to be several carats.

"Joe?" my mother's voice behind me called, allowing me a chance to take a breath.

Joe stood. "Hello, Belinda. Happy Thanksgiving. Hi, Ray."

I turned to see that my sister had also come into the foyer. "Ummm … Joe's here, everyone."

"We see that," my mother said through a chuckle, her gaze falling on the ring in Joe's hand. "Come inside, Joe."

Joe looked at me, but then followed my mother and sister into the kitchen.

I followed behind him, my hands going to my face, wondering how to tell the man I'd lived with for three years that I was in love with another man, in less than two weeks. Well, thirty-three years and two weeks.

Once inside the kitchen, my mother turned back to Joe. "You want coffee or tea, Joe?"

"Coffee'd be great," Joe said, but then he turned back to me, taking my hand in his. "Alaina …" Tears came to my eyes, and he smiled, clearly thinking they were happy tears.

"Mom," I said. "Joe and I have to talk." I paused as I thought about where we could go. What restaurant would be open on Thanksgiving Day? But I definitely had to get him out of the house before —

A tap at the mudroom door sounded at the same time the door creaked open, and the familiar paw sounds clicked across the floor toward me. Markus never waited for one of us to answer the door, of course; he'd earned an open invitation years ago.

I scooped up Buddy. "Hey, Buddy."

Markus approached me, immediately wrapping one arm around me, since his other arm held a wrapped box. "Hey, babe." His arm dropped as he took in the stranger in the kitchen.

"Markus," I said through a gulp, "this is Joe. Joe, this is Markus." Joe snapped the lid of the box closed and stuffed it into his jacket pocket before extending his hand to Markus.

"Hello, Markus."

"Hi, Joe. I'm an old friend of the family. Nice to finally meet you. Did you drive all the way from New York?"

Joe's posture relaxed a bit at Markus's words. Markus had made it sound as though he were nothing more than a family friend, and had addressed Joe as though he were happy to meet him.

Joe stepped forward and possessively wrapped his arm around my waist. "Yeah. Headed out at five this morning. Didn't want to miss spending Thanksgiving with Alaina."

I stepped out of Joe's reach and set Buddy down, then headed to the coffee maker. "Coffee, anyone?" I asked as I turned and held up the pot.

"Sure," Joe chirped, taking a seat at the head of the table.

"That'd be great," Markus said, pulling out a chair at the opposite end of the table. He set the wrapped box he'd brought in with him on the end of the table, then sank into the vinyl-covered chair.

Mom and Raylene sat down on the same side as each other, leaving an entire side for me to sit in between the two men in my life. *Goody.* I wondered if anyone would notice if I slipped some of Mom's Jameson into my cup and then escaped out the back door.

No way had Markus not seen the ring in Joe's hand. And no way had Joe missed the hug and "Babe" comment from Markus.

Dear God … Please open up a sinkhole in the middle of the kitchen so I can escape this nightmare.

"So, Joe," Raylene started, "I thought you moved to Chicago?"

Bless my wonderful sister …

"Well, yes, I did accept an offer, but I'm not sure if I want it if Alaina doesn't want to leave New York."

I carried the cups to the table, setting one in front of Joe and another in front of Markus.

"Hmmm," my sister responded. "But what if Alaina decided to stay here for a while?"

"In Pittsburgh?" Joe asked, his eyes darting up to mine.

"In Squirrel Hill," Raylene corrected him.

I stepped to the empty side of the table opposite my mother and sister, and jumped when the chair closest to Markus suddenly popped out from beneath the table. Markus smiled, but the smile disappeared quickly, replaced by a look in his eye I'd never seen, coupled with a twitch in his jaw. Markus was mad. I'd never seen him mad. And after he'd been so friendly to Joe. The question was … Was he mad at me? Did he expect me to throw Joe out after he'd driven more than six hours?

Joe met my eyes. "I *would* move here if that's what Alaina wants. My company has a branch in Pittsburgh. After being away from Alaina for two weeks, I realized it didn't matter where I lived if she wasn't —"

The screech of a chair cut off Joe's words, and then Markus was on his feet. "I brought this for you, Laina." He slid the box toward me.

"Thank you, Markus," I murmured, not sure what else to say to him. The slight comical side of the situation had staved off my tears, but I felt them fighting for release.

Joe reached for my hand. "Did you hear me, Alaina? I'd move here if it's what you want."

The doorbell rang, and I jumped. "Who else is coming to dinner?" I was on my feet in a second, Buddy on my heels, to answer the door. At this point, I'd answer the door for a vacuum salesman, or even someone carrying religious tracts. A conversation about Heaven and Hell could last hours, which would postpone the conversation waiting to happen in the kitchen. It wasn't that I didn't know what I wanted. I did. I just didn't want to be rude to either of the men in my life. After all, I'd told Markus that I hadn't officially broken up with Joe, even though I was standing by my earlier thought that Joe had been the one to leave me for something better in Chicago.

If I left with Joe to have the conversation I knew I needed to have, Markus would be upset, though. The tightening of his jaw told me that. If I just told Joe to leave without an explanation after three years, then he'd be upset. And I just didn't want to hurt either man.

I swung the door open without bothering to look who was calling, but then slammed my hand over my mouth when I saw who it was. "Howard?"

"Hi, Alaina. I was hoping I had the right house. Can I come in?"

This is the part in the play where I faint and the director yells, "Cut!" But I just stood there staring, wondering why the greatest producer in the world was standing on my doorstep with a bottle of wine in his hands.

Chapter 17 – With Any Luck

Coming out of my shock at seeing Howard Edwards the Second on my front porch, I braced my hands against the doorframe. Did he think he could bully me into taking a role? "Why are you here? I told Michelle that I was sorry, but I simply cannot accept the role due to a family emergency."

"Excuse me?" Howard asked politely.

"The role? I told Michelle I couldn't accept the part. Isn't that why you're here?"

"Howard?" Raylene asked from behind me. The familiar way she said his name had me stepping back to look at her. She approached the two of us. "What are you doing here?"

Howard stepped over the threshold, even though I hadn't invited him inside. "Hi, Ray. It's been a long time." He kissed her cheek, then handed her the bottle of wine. "Happy Thanksgiving, love. I hope you don't mind my stopping by. When I saw Alaina … she and you, other than the hair color, could be twins. I knew she had to be your sister."

A bright red blush rose on my sister's cheeks like I'd never seen. In fact, I couldn't ever remember witnessing a man kissing Raylene on the cheek, even platonically. She just wasn't that kind of woman. She naturally put off a "don't touch" vibe.

"So you *do* know each other," I accused, lifting my head as Markus, Joe, and then Mom stepped into the foyer. No wonder Howard had stared at me outside the theater as if he had known me.

Howard smiled. "Of course we know each other, but it's been …" He looked thoughtful for a moment. "I'd come home on college break, and you'd just graduated. So, twenty-four years …?"

Raylene nodded. "Something like that."

I tilted my head, completely content that someone else's life was on display for the moment instead of mine.

My mother clapped her hands. "Well, the more the merrier. Take off your coat, Howard, and come on into the kitchen. We have room for one more person."

Howard flashed his million-dollar smile. "Love to, Mrs. Ackerman."

I gulped again as Markus caught my eye. "We need to talk," he mouthed.

I simply nodded and then followed my mother into the kitchen.

Markus scooped the wrapped box off the table and then took my hand. "Excuse me, everyone. I need to discuss something with Alaina. We'll be right back."

Joe stepped in our path. "I came here to discuss something with Alaina, as well."

Markus cocked his head and then pointed to himself. "Best friend for thirty-three years. I go first. Then you're welcome to have all the conversation you want."

His hand tightly around mine, Markus pushed past Joe and led me upstairs to my bedroom. Once inside, he started to close the door, until he saw Buddy charging toward it. Markus held it open long enough for Buddy to barrel through, then closed and locked the door in one swift move.

He set the wrapped box on my dresser, then turned to me. He took one step forward, then pulled me into his arms. His mouth pressed hard against mine and, without a thought, I opened up to him, allowing his tongue to touch mine. He pulled back only slightly, then took my top lip and bottom lip, again and again.

"God, I love you, Alaina," he said through his kisses, coaxing me back toward the bed.

"I love you too, Markus, but …"

Markus pulled back. "I wasn't going to try anything. As if I'd want our first time to be when your boyfriend's downstairs. Then again, that might be kind of kinky."

I shoved him back. "That's not what I meant. And Joe's not my boyfriend."

"Sorry, fiancé."

"He's not my fiancé either. He left me. I let him leave. He asked me to go to Chicago, and I said thanks, but no thanks. I think that was answer enough that I didn't love him enough to go further."

Markus sighed. "Then why is he here?"

I closed my eyes. "He says he loves me … that he wants to marry me."

"And do you love him?"

I blew out a breath. "Not enough to marry him."

Markus shuttered his eyes again. "You didn't say no, though."

"Markus, we lived together for three years. Would you rather I had said I lived with a man I didn't love for three years?"

"I don't know ..."

He stood, and I jumped up next to him. "I love you, Markus, and I want to stay here, in Squirrel Hill, with you. I know that. But please don't ask me to be rude to Joe."

Markus pulled me back into his arms. "Are you really going to stay, Laina, even though he's offering you a chance to stay in New York? And probably a twenty-thousand-dollar ring?"

"Even then." I stared up at him. "Twenty thousand? Really? You think it's that expensive? Maybe I should consider a short engagement —"

Markus cut off my silly words with a kiss, then pulled back. "Sit." Buddy sat. "Not you, Buddy, but good boy." Markus petted Buddy on the head and then headed to the dresser. He carried the wrapped box to the bed and set it in front of me. "An early gift."

"But it's not even December ..."

"Open it, Laina."

I pulled on the ribbon, unraveling the red satiny plastic, then set it on the bed. I carefully ripped the gold paper back to reveal a plain white box, about the size of a notebook. Inside, wrapped in tissue paper, was a stack of papers bounded together by a black binder clip.

"Go ahead," Markus urged.

Instead of unclipping the papers, I lifted up the first page to reveal the title, *With Any Luck*. I smiled up at Markus. "That doesn't sound like sci-fi."

"Keep going."

I turned the page. The next page was titled: *Dedication.*
For Alaina, the love of my life.

***With Any Luck**, someday you'll be my
wife.
I wrote this play for you, my love.*

"Markus …" My eyes watered up instantly. "You wrote a play? For me? Wife?"

Markus dropped to his knees. "This wasn't where I planned to do this. I wanted to do it later tonight, when we were all alone, but I'll never let you go again without you knowing how I feel." He lifted my hand off my lap and held it in his. "Will you marry me, Alaina? Someday? It doesn't have to be next week or even next year. We can take all the time you want. But will you be mine, forever?"

"Oh, Markus. Yes, of course, I'll marry you." I sniffed to hold back the tears as he slid the ring onto my finger. It wasn't as grand as the one Joe had offered, but it was perfect. Absolutely perfect.

Markus crawled up on the bed and pulled me into his arms, kissing my forehead, cheeks, nose, then finally my lips again. "I love you."

"I love you, too."

"And how about the play?"

"What do you mean?"

"I want you to star in it. I've been writing it for years, but I've only been able to finish it since you came home. I already showed it to my agent, and he loves it. Thinks he can sell it."

"But …"

"We'll be together."

"But what about Raylene?"

Markus kissed my nose. "After Raylene gets better, baby. These things don't happen overnight."

"You really wrote a play for me?"

"I really did. No one else could play the role, I assure you. It was written just for you."

"Markus, that is quite possibly the most romantic thing anyone has ever done for me."

His cheeks lifted. "You haven't seen anything yet. I have twenty-some years of making up to do. And I'm going to start by kicking your ex-boyfriend out of the house."

"Markus, don't you dare! In fact, you stay here." I slid the ring off my finger, but then glared at him when he narrowed his eyes. "There's just no reason to cause a scene. That ring will go right back on my finger in fifteen minutes. But you're going to give me fifteen minutes, do you hear me? You gave me twenty years to come home to you ... you can give me fifteen more minutes."

"Deal. But if he's not gone in fifteen minutes, I'll help him leave."

"Feisty. I think I like this side of you."

Markus shook his head. "Alaina, you have a skewed image of me, I think. I wasn't as sweet and innocent as you appear to think I was."

"You weren't?"

"No. Not even close." He laughed. "We'll save those stories for later, though. Pillow talk. I'll see you in fifteen minutes. Maybe we can start then —"

I raised my brow. "Aren't you coming downstairs?"

"I don't think that's a good idea. Buddy and I'll wait for you right here. I'd hate to be one of those houses that has a domestic disturbance call on Thanksgiving."

"What are you talking about?" I couldn't imagine Markus doing anything to cause a scene.

"Alaina, didn't you see the way he stepped in between us? Trust me, Joe and I shouldn't be in the same room when you tell him."

I rolled my eyes. "Okay. I'll see you in fifteen minutes."

"We'll be right here." Markus slid down to the floor and scooped Buddy into his lap. He held up the ring. "Hurry, I don't want this ring to ever come off your finger again."

I smiled, then stepped out the door, pulling it behind me.

In the hallway, I couldn't help but laugh. I'd made it to thirty-nine without getting engaged, and now I'd had two men ask me on the same day.

Only one of them was the man I'd been in love with practically my entire life, though.

Oddly enough, it appears Fate knew what she was doing after all. When I thought I was down on my luck, she'd just been re-writing a better scene. The happily-ever-after I always loved in stories would now be mine.

Not just Markus, but my life here in Squirrel Hill, Mom, Raylene, and Buddy were all part of my happily-ever-after.

Chapter 18 – HEA x 2?

Fifteen minutes later, I raced up the steps to my room. Markus and I had forever for pillow talk and to make up kisses … and more. Today was Thanksgiving, and I planned to milk it for all its worth, making up time I'd missed with my mother and sister over the years.

Joe left without argument, telling me that if I ever changed my mind, he'd transfer back to New York, but for now, he'd keep the job in Chicago.

We'd talked outside in Joe's vehicle, so I didn't hear what Howard, Raylene, and my mother were doing. But Howard was still there, as indicated by the beautiful Audi S5 in the driveway.

I opened the door to my room, but paused in the doorway.

Markus was lying back on the bed, playing on his phone. It reminded me of when we were seventeen. He looked up at me with those bright green eyes. "Is he gone?"

"Yes." I laughed.

"Then come here." He held his arms open, an irresistible request.

I bounded across the floor and leapt into the bed. "We can't stay here long, you know ..."

"I know." He lifted my hand and slipped the ring back on my ring finger, kissing my hand. Then he lifted his head and locked eyes with me. "I love you, Alaina. Thank you for finally making my dreams come true."

"It's been my dream, too, Markus. I just let other things get in the way."

Markus cupped his hand around the back of my neck and pulled me to him. His lips met mine, and I melted into him.

Breathless after his kiss, remembering our night in his truck twenty years ago, I pulled back. "You know ... I should have known."

"Known what?"

"That you weren't as pure as I imagined. Sweet boys don't do ... you know ... what you did to me twenty years ago."

His mouth turned up in his widest grin. "You've thought about that, have you?"

"All the time." I sighed.

"Maybe ..." He kissed me softly. "If you don't have any plans. Maybe we could make this a short engagement, and get right to the honeymoon."

"That sounds perfect."

He pulled back. "Really?"

"Really. I don't want to plan a large wedding with Ray being so sick. What if we just got married now, and then we can have an actual wedding ceremony after she feels well again?"

Markus nodded. "I like the way you think, Alaina Ackerman. Okay, let's go hang out with the family, and then we'll start creating some new holiday traditions." He pulled me into his arms and then slid off the bed, standing with me cradled in his arms. "I definitely have a lot to give thanks for."

He stood me up and we walked downstairs, Buddy on our heels.

In the kitchen, Raylene was sitting across from Howard, and Mom was stirring something on the stove.

"Guess what, Laina?" Raylene said as soon as Markus and I stepped near the table. "Howard just told me that other than one scene in West Virginia, the entire movie will be filmed in and around Pittsburgh."

I looked at Markus and then Howard. "Yeah, but I still need to be home."

My sister glared at me. "We'll discuss what you need to do later. I just wanted you to know."

Got it. Obviously, she didn't want to tell Howard about the cancer. "So, you and Howard …"

Howard laughed. "It's been a long time, but I couldn't resist. I was here visiting my parents anyway."

"Have you guys dated?" I asked.

Howard and Ray exchanged a look, but my sister spoke. "Not exactly …" Raylene's eyes dropped to my hand. "Laina!" My mother turned at the excitement in Raylene's tone. And then Raylene scooted back in her chair. "Come let me see. Is that what I think it is?"

Now Mom was beside me. "Oh, honey! I thought it would never happen!" Mom grabbed Markus and squeezed him before she hugged me. "You two will make the best couple ever."

Raylene stood and hugged me, then Markus. "Congratulations, you two."

Howard stood next. "Congratulations!" Then his gaze met Raylene's. "I should get back to the house." Raylene nodded. Howard turned to me. "Alaina, we'll talk Monday. I'm sure we can work out something."

"Thanks," I said, then nodded for Raylene to walk Howard to the door.

Raylene had done a great job of turning the focus off her and Howard to me, but there was definitely something there.

Maybe my sister would get her happily-ever-after too.

It's never the end, as there's always one more story to share...

If you haven't read *Some Lucky Woman (Jana's Story)*, turn the page for a sneak peek, or just head on over to my website, www.CarmenDeSousaBooks.com, for links to all of my books.

Sneak Peek

Book Description

Some lucky women meet the man of their dreams and live happily ever after. Some lucky women focus on a career and make their own happily ever after. And then some women wake up after fifteen years of marriage and discover that their luck just ran out … right into the arms of another woman.

Jana Embers isn't one to sit back, though. The first thing Jana realizes she needs to do is empty the joint bank account, then she's thinking she might take a tire iron to her soon-to-be-ex-husband's truck. After that, she's not sure what she'll do … Maybe she'll adopt a cat.

After her divorce and too many crummy dates, Jana decides she doesn't need a man. A perfectly sized and shaped device and writing about the perfect hero will more than suffice. Determined to share her philosophy, she pens *You Don't Need a Man*, encouraging women everywhere to go out and experience life instead of waiting for a man to complete them.

Three years later, Jana has a *New York Times* bestseller and a contract for a movie adaptation, but she also has a shoulder injury, which has put a crimp in her new carefree lifestyle. Worse yet, she can't write. Her only hope is Dr. Adrian Kijek, a renowned physical therapist who hates her simply because she wrote a book about not needing a man, or so she thinks …

Some Lucky Woman

Jana's Story

"To love oneself is the beginning of a life-long romance."
— Oscar Wilde

Chapter 1 – Temporary Insanity

Temporary insanity, I thought as I swung the tire iron I'd plucked out of my Toyota Tacoma against the headlights of my husband's four-wheel-drive Tundra. I felt bad for hurting such a beautiful truck, but I'd done everything for that lying, cheating, two-timing son-of-a-bitch, and this was the only way I could think of to hurt him.

Certainly, even a fresh-out-of-college attorney could get a jury of my peers to understand why I had to take revenge against Dick Embers. And since I didn't have the stomach to pull a "Lorena Bobbitt" job, a "Carrie Underwood" meltdown would have to suffice.

Maybe that would be my defense ... *She'd been listening to the radio, Your Honor,* my attorney would plead on my behalf, *and well, the next thing Jana Embers knew, she'd come to with a tire iron —*

"Jana!" my husband's shrill tone hit me just as I smashed in the second taillight. "Oh, my God! Are you insane?"

I looked up at my soon-to-be ex-husband and forced a smile. "As a matter of fact, I am. Meet your creation, Dick!" I swung the heavy steel rod down on the lip of the tailgate, leaving an indentation that no dent-remover tool in the world would ever be able to pull out.

Dick Embers pressed his clenched fists to his head as he assessed the damage, but then stopped gawking and chased me as I ran to the front of the truck. "Give me the tire iron, Jana," he said as calmly as I'd ever heard him speak.

I swung the heavy metal against the hood. "Fifteen years! I've given you everything within me for fifteen years. And you repay me by getting some bimbo pregnant."

Dick raised his hand as though he expected me to hand him my weapon. "It was a mistake, Jana. I didn't mean —"

"A mistake?" I swung my makeshift bat into the chrome grille as though all the bases were loaded and I was going for a home run. "Wearing different color socks is a mistake." *Whack.* "Sending a text to the wrong person is a mistake." *Whack.* "Sticking your penis in the wrong woman isn't a mistake, *Dick*!"

He dropped his head. "I'm sorry —"

"Sorry?" I jabbed at a piece of dangling metal that hadn't fallen. "Sorry because you got caught? Sorry because you didn't use a condom?" My eyes on him, I backed up to the driver's door, hopped up on the running board, and then bashed the windshield with all my might. "I made you who you are, Dick Embers. If it wasn't for me, you never would have been promoted at that stupid car dealership. I handled all of your follow-up calls for your work and still found time to wash and cook and clean. I changed all the diapers, handled all the discipline for our son …" I continued to bring down the iron rod on the front window over and over, aggravated that the safety glass refused to shatter. "We had sex all the time, as often as you wanted …"

Dick took a step toward me, so I jumped off the side step and held the tire rod on my shoulder, ready to swing it against his head if he came near me. *Self-defense*, my attorney would call it. *Mrs. Jana Embers was in fear of her life after she'd gone temporarily insane.*

"Please, Jana," Dick whined.

"Please, what?" I screeched.

"Please forgive me."

"And have to share you with a woman for the next eighteen years while the child the two of you adulterers created grows up? No. Uh-uh. Not this woman, Dick. I gave you fifteen years. I'm certainly not stupid enough to give you another day."

I walked backward in the direction of my Tacoma, surprised to see that every corridor of the apartment building where Dick had moved into this week had people standing in the doorways.

Ignoring the surrounding stares, wondering why no one had called the police yet, I raised my chin to Dick as I opened the door. "Oh, I'll be filing for divorce first thing in the morning."

The crowd cheered, some whistled, one woman called out, "Atta girl!"

Surprised, I twirled my weapon as though it were a baton and curtsied. I skipped to my truck and hopped inside, feeling the most alive I'd felt my entire life.

Shaking too violently to avoid spillage, I used both of my hands to lift a cup of coffee to my lips, wondering when the police would show up. The adrenaline from my crazed attack on Dick's Tundra had worn off, replaced with the fear that I might be spending the next sixty days in jail.

I'd called my cousin on my way home in case I needed someone to drive my fifteen-year-old son to school and then be available to bail me out of jail. Now we just sat across from each other, staring in silence, fearing the rap on the door that would surely come at any moment. I'd never been incarcerated before. I wasn't very large. So how would I defend myself in jail? I wondered briefly if the arresting officer would let me take my tire iron. Probably not. Especially since it would be marked as exhibit *A* on the evidence table.

Angela reached for my quivering hands. "I'm so sorry, Jana. Is there anything I can do? Is there something else you need to handle? Not that I can beat up a truck or anything."

A laugh burst out of my mouth that quickly turned into a sob. "No … but … thank you. Before I went on my rampage, I went online and transferred every penny out of our joint accounts, which sadly wasn't as much as I'd hoped. I dumped every penny into Eric's account, since it was the only account that didn't have Dick's name on it. Then I called all our credit card companies, reported the cards as lost, and ordered new cards. I'm not sure what else I can do."

"So this is really happening?" Angela asked.

I swiped at my tears. "What else was I supposed to do, Ang? Not only did he cheat on me, but he also didn't use protection. God only knows what type of disease that woman might have … or any other woman he might have been screwing."

Angela blew out a long breath. "You've just been together so long. Heck, you've been married since I was in grade school. I've known Dick almost my entire life."

"Yeah … me too," I said on a sigh. "Since I was nineteen. Believe me, I didn't plan to be a single mother at thirty-four. And what will I do to make money? I have a B.A. in business, but what good is that when I haven't worked outside the home in fifteen years? I've spent nearly half of my life helping him make it to the top. And then he —" I burst into tears again, as I'd been doing for the last week. It surprised me that I had enough water left in my body to shed any more tears.

Angela got up from her chair and wrapped her arms around me. "I'm so sorry, Jana. I really am. I wish there was something I could say or do that would make you feel better."

I sniffed and looked up at my cousin, who also happened to be my best friend. "Ever think about contract killing?"

Angela laughed. "No, and I'm going to forget that you asked that."

"Okay, so if you won't kill him, the least you could do is help me figure out how to get back at him. And give me some suggestions of what I can do to make money. I did a budget last night, and even if Dick continues to pay the mortgage, and I scrimp and scrape every dime, I have enough savings to pay for the utilities and food for about a year. After that, I'll have to hit the streets."

"From what you told me last night, I think you already got back at him." Angela sat back down, then picked up her mug, smiling over her steaming hot latte. "You still look pretty good, too. I'm nine years younger than you and I have more gray hairs than you do. Maybe it's the dark shade you got from your mom, whereas I got the light hair from your father and my dad's side of the family. I bet you'd do rather well on the streets."

I rolled my eyes, then swiped at my tears again. "Not funny, Ang. Seriously. It's not like I can go back to cocktail waitressing. Who wants to see a thirty-four-year-old mom in short-shorts and a tank top?"

My cousin jumped up from her chair. "I got it! Remember when I told you about Jenny, my friend from college who's doing so well, the one who started that couponing website."

I dropped my head into my palm, rubbing my temples with my middle finger and thumb, trying to massage away a headache that was forming from lack of sleep ... and stress ... and probably because I hadn't eaten anything in days. Not to mention that the continuous waterworks had more than likely left me dehydrated. "I don't even like clipping coupons for myself."

Angela waved her hands as she paced around my kitchen. "It's more than that. It's not really about the coupons as much as it is about the products she displays on her website. She's an affiliate for several major websites. And get this," Angela leaned across the counter in front of me, "she makes up to ten percent when someone from her site buys a product, any product. It doesn't even have to be the item she's advertising."

I sniffed, then cocked my head. "Go on ..."

"Well, you just have to find something you love, and then start blogging about it. From there, I guess you can add all the links."

I huffed out a breath. "What do I love? I've never done anything. I know how to be a wife and mother. Other than that, I don't even have any hobbies. I've been too busy raising Eric and taking care of my stupid unfaithful husband."

Ignoring my complaint, Angela slid onto a barstool, then rested her head on her folded hands. "There's gotta be something, Jana."

"I like wine ..." I ventured, thinking a tall goblet of Merlot would taste really good about now, but Angela would probably start to question me if I pulled out a bottle of wine at five a.m. "You and I have always enjoyed going to those wine-tasting events. And I'm great at picking out the most expensive."

Angela nodded, then shook her head. "You are, but I don't think that's a good idea. You know, with your mother's history ... and Aunt Heidi."

I didn't want to think about my mother. Not that I knew her anyway. She'd been dead since I was in diapers. My aunt, on the other hand, had been the closest thing to a mother I'd known. But in the last year or so, I'd only seen her a handful of times. Angela and I both knew she had a drinking problem, but it seemed to have gotten worse lately.

Not that I was an alcoholic, but with the history of drug and alcohol abuse in both of my parents' families, it probably wouldn't be a good idea to take up a hobby that required me to drink on a daily basis.

"Yeah ... I guess you're right," I said.

"Oh!" Angela jumped up again. Even pregnant, the woman had more energy than my son, and that was saying a lot. "Reading! You love to read!" she exclaimed with conviction, as though my love of reading would solve all of my problems. Truly, reading had helped me cope when I was a teenager, but I doubted I could disappear into make believe as I'd done when I was an adolescent.

Still trying to loosen the tension in my head, I pinched the skin above my eyebrow. "Yeah, but how am I going to make money from reading?"

"You can blog about what you read. Write reviews and stuff."

"Angela, you're a lot younger than I am. You understand all of that computer stuff. I wouldn't know how to do that."

"Jenny says it's easy. In fact, she's been wanting to train me. But with the baby, not to mention being pregnant again, I just don't have the time or energy. I'm sure she'd come over and help you set it up, though, especially if you tell her you'll link back to her site."

I leaned back in my chair. It was worth a look. I didn't like the idea of starting a full-time job when Eric was accustomed to me taking him to school and all of his extra-curricular activities every day. Since I'd been unable to do much other than go to school and babysit Angela when I was a teenager, I'd wanted Eric to enjoy his high school years.

"Okay … I'll look into it. Anything is better than nothing at this point, I guess. Besides, it'll give me something to do so I don't spend every minute of my day scheming how to make Dick's life a living hell."

Angela laughed. "Well, it's been three hours and the police haven't shown up. Maybe he's decided not to press charges, hoping he'll get in your good graces."

I inhaled a deep breath, hoping Angela was right about the cops, but then said, "Dick Embers couldn't earn his way back into my good graces if he were the Pope himself.

—

Thank you for reading this sneak peek.

Please look for *Some Lucky Woman* on my website, www.CarmenDeSousaBooks.com.

Before you go …

I hope you enjoyed *Down on Her Luck*. If you haven't already, please stop by my website, www.CarmenDeSousaBooks.com, to find links to all of my books.

If you enjoyed *Down on Her Luck*, please check out my other books. Although all of my stories have a common thread — Love and Forgiveness — I write in several genres: Romantic Suspense, Paranormal Romantic Suspense, and Mysteries with a Paranormal Edge.

The Southern Romantic-Suspense collection consists of five stand-alone stories — NO CLIFFHANGERS — but a couple of them should be read before the follow-up novels, so as not to run into spoilers. You can read them in any order, as long as you read Charlotte 1 before Charlotte 2 and Nantahala 1 before Nantahala 2.

The *Creatus* Series, an Urban Fantasy / Paranormal Romance series, on the other hand should be read in order.

I also write a collection of mysteries with a ghostly edge.

You can find all my books on my website,
www.CarmenDeSousaBooks.com.

If you enjoyed *Down on Her Luck*, please leave a review. It doesn't have to be fancy, just a few words to let other readers know if they should download it too. It means so much to an author to hear what readers loved — even didn't love — about a book. It's how we grow and learn what you want to read next time … and in the case of a series, which characters you want to see more of in the next books or which ones we should knock off. :)

Thank you again!

Carmen